Come Back to Bed, Beautiful

Mayton Hearts, Volume 1

Abigail Bay

Published by Lady Hatwick, 2023.

This book is dedicated to Helen, for a laugh.

And for all the laughs.

Come Back to Bed, Beautiful
Book 1, Mayton Hearts series
Published by AG Spiers imprint Lady Hatwick
Wellington, New Zealand
Cover design by AG Spiers
ISBN 978-0-473-61854-4 (EPUB)
ISBN 978-0-473-61855-1 (Kindle)
ISBN 978-0-473-61853-7 (Hardcover POD)
ISBN 978-0-473-61852-0 (Softcover POD)
Requests to publish work from this book should be made to:
abigailbay.author@gmail.com

Chapter 1

I take my flight in total silence, lost in the noise in my head. I wonder if I am fleeing from something, or towards something. And if it even matters. Jeffrey is far behind me. The glittering coastline of a new country is before me and there is the deep, comforting thought of my novel – unwritten as yet but perfect, full of hope and potential in my tired, aching, frightened heart.

At Wellington Airport I expect to see my sister Lori, but there is no one to meet me. I wait in the collection area with a growing sense of alarm, until it is obvious no one is coming for me. I have never been to New Zealand before, I barely even know Lori, and I have no idea what to do next.

I take a firm grip on my suitcase and head outside to look for her. Beyond the glass doors there is a cold wind. It nips my ankles and whips my shoulder-length hair across my face. I feel suddenly forlorn. I have changed my life irrevocably in coming here, yet there is no welcome, no fanfare, just an odd sense of failure. I stand irresolute, my stomach churning, as a brief flurry of passengers swirls around me.

The crowd fades and I am left alone. I am distantly aware of a large vehicle noise but I am worried now, upset, I want to look for Lori's car. I haul my suitcase off the kerb and step out across a narrow service road.

With a deafening hiss of air brakes, an enormous truck screeches to a stop, its towering chrome bullbar barely a foot from my head. I jump back, falling over my Louis Vuitton, and scramble for the kerb.

"Look out!" The voice is masculine, brusque with shock. "Bloody hell, lady, I almost killed you!"

Startled and embarrassed, I can't look at him. *Well done, Kate! Why not get run over on your first day in New Zealand?* It occurs to me it would be a fitting end to my crazy, messed up life.

Sunlight glances off the truck's chrome trim, dazzling me as I tilt my face to the cab. "I'm sorry, I don't know what I was thinking. It's been a long day."

There is a pause. "You sound English. Are you English?" He sighs. "Of course, it'd have to be you – tell me, is your name Kate?"

"Pardon?"

"Are you Kate Dale, Lorien Henare's sister?"

"Yes!" I shade my eyes with my hand, trying to see the driver. I am stunned. I don't know anyone in New Zealand except Lori.

The driver is swinging down from the cab. "I suppose this is one way to find you. You don't look anything like her, and you've got less road sense, I reckon."

"We're half-sisters, our father was... Look here, you don't have to be rude!"

"And we don't have to be friends." He jumps off the truck step with easy grace and reaches for my suitcase. "Not immediately. I reserve judgement about people who go round jumping in front of trucks." He is tall and lean, with tousled, dark hair. His eyes are the colour of chocolate and there is measured strength in his gaze.

My stomach flutters with the long-forgotten tickle of attraction and I am shocked. I had thought that was forever buried. *Seriously, Katie, you must be so jetlagged!*

I stare at him, wondering if he is joking or serious, and realise he really *is* gorgeous. The kind of drop dead gorgeous that could turn me into an incoherent, blithering wreck if I was actually looking for a man. Which I'm not. And I don't think I ever will again, after...

I clear my throat and muster some stranger danger to avoid swooning into his arms, right here in the service lane. Hands on hips, I open my mouth. "Nngkk." I blush the colour of my suitcase and try again. "Uh, how do you know my name?"

"I'm a friend of Lori and Gus." He shrugs, lazy amusement in his eyes. "They asked me to pick you up. If you check your phone, Lori's probably texted you about it."

I check my phone. Lori has texted me about it. Her son has fallen out of a tree and she's had to take him to hospital for X-rays, so she asked her friend Linc to collect me.

I look at the Kenworth towering above us. "Is this your truck?"

Lori's friend Linc is stowing my luggage. "No, it belongs to Gus. I was collecting it for him from the port today. When Lori couldn't come, it made sense for me to grab you on the same trip."

"Grab me?" I am beginning to wonder about Lori's choice of friends.

"Well, not exactly *grab* you. It's a figure of speech." There is a glint in his eye and I give him a nervous smile, all my anxiety flooding back. "I'm sorry," he says, stepping down again and extending his hand. "Let's start again. Kia ora, Kate. Welcome to New Zealand. I'm Lincoln Brady."

I shake his hand carefully, and he says, "Sweet," but it sounds like an acknowledgement, not an endearment. A smile steals into his eyes and he nods at the truck. "You know, Lori would've killed me if I'd actually hit you with this thing."

"I know." I grimace. I have only met my sister once, when she visited Sydney, but she seems pretty forthright and fearless.

"Gus, too, if you'd dented the chromework."

Now I know he is laughing at me. I turn away and hastily follow my suitcase into the cab.

Inside, the vehicle is all panelling and polish, a beautiful truck. It conjures a sudden childhood memory for me of riding in my father's lorry with its gleaming, walnut dashboard and leather seats. I am surprised I can remember it so clearly, I must have been only four or five years old. With the long flight and my removal to New Zealand, and the nagging ache in my heart, this is all too much. I want to curl up in my seat and cry.

My chest burning, my throat tight, I stare out the window as Linc swings into the driver's seat. He brings the scent of mountains, leather and shaving soap to the cab. I find it inexplicably divine. I embrace the distraction, breathing deeply as he slides the Kenworth into gear and moves slowly away from the kerb.

Have you lost your mind? Get yourself together, Kate.
Ooh, Katie, he's cute!

"Do you need anything before we leave town?" Linc interrupts my thoughts as we leave the airport and join the flow of city traffic.

"Huh?" I am lost in my memories and the voices in my head.

He looks bemused. "Hungry? Thirsty? We've a bit of a drive ahead."

"No, thankyou. I ate earlier. I think I just need sleep, more than anything."

"Nothing to stop you." He leans over and I flinch, but he is reaching behind me into the sleeping compartment. He drags out a pillow. "Here. It will take us a few hours to reach Lori's farm."

I stare at him. "Thankyou."

"All good." And he settles in to drive, his entire focus now apparently on the road. I wait but he doesn't say anything else, so I lean on the pillow against the glass and let the scenery roll by.

From Wellington city, Linc steers us around the coast and through the faultline-forged Hutt Valley, lying north-south straight as a die. The truck's wheels spin down Highway 2, following its curves into the foothills and over the hunched shoulders of the Remutaka Range. Linc is silent and I am left to my thoughts. Half-dozing, I wonder if he senses my pensiveness. I'm not sure I can ascribe much sensitivity to this man, he hasn't said much and his first words were to scold me. Then I remember the pillow, and frown.

I look outside at the hills, cast golden in the fading light. I watch the truck's shadow flitting alongside, and marvel at the unknown trees and jagged hills of my new home.

We arrive at Lori's farm just on dusk. The farm is isolated and Lori is still out, her house dark and unwelcoming. I tap at my cellphone but there is a scant bar of reception here and no new message from Lori.

Linc hesitates, the truck burbling gutturally in Lori's driveway. I can't tell if he is annoyed by the delay, or resigned. "Do you know if you are staying at Lori's place, or in the old homestead?"

I pull a crumpled note from my pocket and read awkwardly, "Is that Way-, Why-..."

"Waiata. That's the original homestead for this farm. Named after the Māori word for a song or a chant." He rubs at his jaw and comes to a decision. "I'll take you straight there. You can get settled in, and Lori will find you when she gets back." He swings the truck smoothly round the circle drive, turns left and rumbles on up a gravel track, hauling us deeper into the farm.

My new home is an old, weatherboard farmhouse nestled at the end of a large, treed paddock. As we approach, I expect to feel some kind of excitement but the place just looks cold and lonely. There is a big, unlit bay window, verandahs, a whitewashed chimney over the tin roof, and shadowy pines beyond. I open the truck door and cool, pine-scented air rushes in.

Linc jumps down and totes my luggage onto the back porch. "Back door will be open," he says briskly. "It always is, here. If you want to lock up, the key will be on the sill."

I am staring at the house. "The garden looks overgrown – wild, almost." I can't tell in this darkness if I love it or hate it.

"She's an old house but she has a good heart." He hesitates a moment in the gathering twilight. "Are you alright?"

Not *will* you be alright, but *are* you. I bristle. *Does he know something about me?* "Yes, of course."

"I know Gus is in Taranaki overnight, and Lori must have been held up with something important. She wouldn't have wanted to miss you."

"Yes." I suddenly want him gone. With his gorgeous eyes and his solicitousness, he confuses me.

"I could help bring in your..." Linc leans reflexively to lift my luggage again.

"No!" I take a deep breath. "No. Thankyou." I'd rather he was still a brusque and offhand stranger – not this handsome man with kind eyes, enquiring if I'm OK.

Linc gives me a long look, then a smile. "Alright. Goodnight, Kate Dale." He swings into the cab, fires up the engine and rolls off down the driveway. I stand in the sudden darkness and feel the night close in around me.

This is your new home, Katie.

I step onto the worn timber boards by the back door and run my hand along the wrinkled paintwork of the nearest sill. I open the door of faded blue to reveal a gloomy hallway beyond. There are signs of a kitchen and living rooms to the left, bathroom on the right, then a right-angled turn, presumably leading to bedrooms. Moonlight filters through the tall windows ahead, and musty air speaks of a large, rambling house long left empty. There is a tumble of firewood beside me in the porch and the glint of starlight on glass. I breathe in the night air and find it full of blossom scent, pine shavings and dust.

I feel abandoned, yet I came here of my own free will. I feel lost, yet I hope to find something. Anything.

I am terrified.

This is perfect.

Out on the highway, Linc gives the Kenworth her head. He feels the powerful truck engine surge, barrelling through the Wairarapa night towards his home. His gaze is focussed on the twin headlights scything between the fencelines, dashing over the intermittent white lines reflecting in his eyes.

He feels angry, worried, thoughtful. Is it possible to be all those things at once?

Kate Dale. She'd impressed him at first sight, so small in stature, with bobbed, honey-coloured hair and startling green eyes. She'd stepped off that kerb like she was about to take on the whole world. Yet after his initial shock at almost running her over, he'd sensed fragility in her. When he'd joked around, she looked at him like he might eat her. She had seemed so sad in the cab, and she'd flinched when he reached to get the pillow.

Why had she flinched? Had she imagined he would hurt her? Linc felt terrible. It was not like he could straight up ask about something like that, so he'd made no comment at the time, but he'd thought about it most of the way to Lori's place.

Now he shifts down a gear to approach a junction, and grimaces. Linc is aware that Kate is not his type. He has always gone for confident women, women with a bounce in their step and a sparkle in their eyes, who will tell him exactly what they want. He knows where he is with that. And he's definitely not looking for anyone – he's got Sue to think about.

But, as he veers right at the junction towards home, he can't get her out of his head.

When I walk into Lorien's old homestead, the first thing I notice is the silence. The second thing is the sheer darkness of night. I've just come from inner city Sydney, where the glare of lights and roar of traffic has been a constant in my life. The incoherent rumble of engines, wheeze of brakes and occasional siren has backfilled my every thought and moment. There, I was surrounded by hundreds, thousands, millions of people, all of us inhabiting the same humming, breathing beast of a city as it sprawled gracelessly from Bondi to the Blue Mountains, trailing glittering tendrils north and south.

And I grew up in London.

To be exposed to silence here, to the rawness of nature and open space without city trappings around me, is shocking. A nature, too, that I do not recognise. The trees seem different here, thicker, darker, the bush gullies too dense to walk through. The homestead garden appears to loom outside my windows. My life is filled with an endless sense of space tonight and I feel threatened.

I muster my courage and set out to explore the house, switching on lights as I go. I leave them all burning – the bare bulb by the back door, the carriage lamps on the front verandah, the living room lights ablaze so they spill through the French doors and the bay window, setting the unkempt rose garden aglow.

I find there are four bedrooms, one with a little ensuite. I name them each Lavender, Rose, Sunflower and Bluebell, according to their faded wallpapers. I feel too restless to choose one, so I will take turns sleeping in each.

I plump up some pillows on the big old bed in Bluebell, the smallest of the rooms, and climb in, still wearing my clothes. I lie there, trying not to think, visually tracing the decorative plaster on the high ceiling over and over, until I know the patterns intimately.

When I sleep at last, it is fitful. I jump awake every time a breeze gusts through the pines or rattles the windowpanes. I feel raw, exposed, and it isn't all due to the wreckage I've made of my life.

In the morning, Lori turns up full of apologies. She explains that her eldest son had fractured his wrist falling out of the tree and she'd spent the entire afternoon in hospital while it was assessed and treated.

I am so happy to see her I lean into her hug and ask, almost desperately, if she'll stay for a cup of tea. Lori has left some supplies in my kitchen for my arrival, so she says cheerily that of course she'll stay.

Lori is smiling and I think then that she is beautiful as I stand there, smiling too. Lori inherited our Māori father's height and dark eyes, and her mother's wavy, auburn hair, which she wears in a ponytail. I am much shorter and honey blonde, with the green eyes and more solid build of my English/Irish mother. We are half-sisters, alike in little ways and yet not, still tentatively building a relationship now we've found each other after so many years.

There is a garish, 1950's dining set in the big farmhouse kitchen and Lori perches there while I make the tea. The gas cooker is temperamental and the teapot big enough to serve an entire shearing team, but I manage. I set out tea in mismatched mugs while Lori chatters about her family, their new truck, and the farm.

"Are your boys at school today?" I ask, setting a plate of shortbread on the table.

"Oh, no, it's school holidays, they're home for another four weeks." Lori rolls her eyes. "I sent them the long way round the farm, that's all, they should be here right about..." And there is a sudden outbreak of scuffling and yelling at the back door as three boys tumble into the hall.

They elbow each other and shove, each trying to be first into the kitchen. "I'm da first!"

"No, *me* da first!"

"You were both last. *I* was first."

"No way! Oh, hi auntie Kate. Yook, Nikki an' Tommo, here's auntie Kate!"

"Hi, auntie Kate," chorus the other two.

"Hello, boys." I am surprised at the sheer energy and chaos that the three boys bring as they bounce in and head straight for the biscuits. The tallest boy, Tommo, has a plaster cast on his arm and he appears already well adjusted to it. Three-year old twins, Nikau and Taika, scramble into my lap for a brief, chaotic hug, perhaps also to get closer to the shortbread plate.

Lori deftly supervises the rationing, mediates between the twins when they think they've been shortchanged a biscuit, then sends them all outside to look for plums in the orchard.

She turns back to me. "That'll give us five minutes, if we're lucky. Now tell me, what did you think of Lincoln?" She peers at me over the rim of her mug.

"Um..." I'm not sure why she's asking, and I feel like a deer in the headlights.

Lori laughs. "It wasn't a trick question, Kate! It's just that Linc can be a bit abrupt and I wondered if he was on his best behaviour, like I told him he should." She sounds amused, almost sisterly, and I wonder at Linc's relationship with Lori and Gus. Is he an employee or a friend? Maybe it's both, in this small-town life.

"Oh. Well, he was polite enough." *After he got over almost hitting me with the truck*. "To be honest, he didn't say much."

"Well, if he does it's worth listening to. Especially if you like horses. He is an absolute legend with horses, and my boys love him."

I like horses, I think, musingly – but in typical Lori fashion she is off now on another topic, laughing about her boys' antics in hospital while the burly, male nurse plastered Tommo's arm. She says Nikau is now obsessed with playing nurse dressups and keeps trying to 'fix' his brothers.

I have time to relax a little. It's not like I need to worry about what she thinks of Lincoln. After Jeffrey, I've sworn off men completely. I am here to rest, heal and write. I have no time for a man, and no interest in one.

Sue swings into the sunlit breakfast room of Summer Homestead, her blonde hair still damp from the shower, her tone light. "Rae rang this morning to chat. She said there's someone moving into the Waiata Homestead, a relative of Lori and Gus. Do you know who it is?"

"A woman called Kate Dale." Linc is buttering toast and doesn't look up. "I dropped her off there last night."

"Oh?" Sue's attention is arrested. "What's she like?"

About your age. Cute as a button. Scared of me. "I think she's Lori's sister, but she doesn't look much like her." He pauses. "I nearly ran her over with Gus's truck."

Sue grins. "So, you haven't lost your usual charm, Linc darling!"

Linc raises an eyebrow. "I'm not trying to charm anyone, Suse. I'm perfectly happy here with you and Brick." He looks down at the Labrador lying at his feet and is whacked by a wagging tail. "See? Brick is happy, too."

Brick rolls upside down, begging, and Sue laughs. "I don't know what I've done to deserve you both."

Linc hands her toast and coffee. Sue pours them both orange juice. After a while, Sue muses, "It'll be good for the old place, to have someone in it."

"Yes."

And nothing more is said of Kate – but Linc heads off to the farm still thinking about her.

Chapter 2

Lady Hatwick is everything I am not. She is tall and buxom with lively, golden ringlets and a husky, mesmerising voice. She is charming. She is confident. She is bold. As I tentatively dip my toes in the waters of my new life at Waiata Homestead, with its creaking floorboards and sprawling garden, Lady Hatwick unfurls, phantomlike, from my laptop and establishes herself in my heart and imagination.

I wonder – no, perhaps hope! – that in time I can borrow some of her character.

At the quiet click of the door latch, she lifts her head from the rumpled pillows and presses one hand to her breast. Her heart quickens when she sees that it is him.

He too has not slept. He, also, has recalled their frenzied meeting in the drawing room and tossed unsatisfied in his bed, until he found himself drawn inexorably to her chamber. His eyes now meet hers, glowing and intense in the candlelight. He lifts an eyebrow in silent query.

She rises from the tangled sheets, shakes back her golden hair and loosens the ribbon of her gown with swift, sure fingers. Lace slips over her shoulder and trails across her breast, making her skin shiver and her nipples swell erect.

He hastens forward, reaching for her with strong hands. His lips meet hers urgently, hungrily, and his body...

"Hello?"

I start at the sound of his voice, strong, clear, and startlingly out of place in Lady Hatwick's crimson-papered bedchamber. I nearly fall off the old chair. *Bloody hell, it's Lincoln!* I click 'Save' and quickly snap down the laptop lid, jumping to my feet like a naughty schoolgirl caught writing graffiti in the loo.

"Hello," I bleat huskily. "In the office. Um, the dining room!"

I hear Linc kick off his boots in the back porch and stroll down the hall. He leans his head round the door. My heart is hammering.

"Mornin'," he says. He catches sight of my face – it feels beetroot red – and he gives me a funny look. "Sorry, am I interrupting something? I can come back later."

"No, I..." I feel my face flush hotter. I cannot possibly tell him that I'm in the middle of writing about steamy infidelity, that I'm trying to work out just how Lady Hatwick would like it best, and what to call handsome Duke Everland's huge, throbbing...

"Try Dick," says Linc.

"Oh, that won't do... What?" I blink and stare at him in astonishment.

"Dick," he repeats patiently. "Dick Trelaney. You mentioned the other night that the garden needed trimming and he's the man, he has a weed eater."

"A weed, er... Oh, yes! The thing that mows grass, the long thing on a..." I stop talking and lean weakly against my desk. "Trelaney, you say?"

"He lives on the Rowan farm. I gave him a call, he can drop round tomorrow. Will you be here?"

Yes, I think to myself, I'll be wrestling with Lady Hatwick's guilt complex by then. So, I nod.

"Sweet," he says. "I can't help 'cos I'm drilling a bore at old Carmichael's place but don't worry, young Dick's primo, he'll do the job alright."

"Primo?"

"Sweet as."

"Oh." I'm still in the dark about what 'primo' means, but this confusion is more welcome than my earlier, cheek-flaming mess. I'm unfamiliar with the Kiwi vernacular. Maybe 'primo' is like 'premium cat food' or premium cut meat. I blink at the fleeting, mental image of Linc's hands gliding over Lady Hatwick's soft skin, interposed with cute lambs leaping about, 'premium quality' stickers plastered to their sides.

Kate, you're losing it.

I frown at the voice in my head. "Thanks for ringing him but you know I could have done it myself. I'm not helpless."

He gives me a light, quizzical smile. "Did I say you were helpless?" His bare arms are brown, his jeans dusty blue against the cream doorframe.

I lift my chin. "Not as such."

"Alright then." Linc pushes himself away from the wall and heads for the back door. He whistles as he pulls on his boots and takes the porch steps two at a time.

I stare after him. *The other night?* Two weeks have gone by since Linc dropped me here and I mentioned the overgrown garden, but he doesn't seem to have noticed. Perhaps time passes differently here.

And why were you so rude, Katie?

"Bye," I say, but needlessly, for Linc has already gone. I cross to the French doors to watch him go, and see him untying a horse from the orchard gate. That's why I hadn't heard him coming. Maybe I need a dog, to help guard against more awkward surprises. Yes, something yappy.

That thought is quickly quashed as I feel the silence of the house settle gently around me again. To my writer's mind it has become a warm, welcoming silence, and I imagine that it would be disturbed forever by the whuffling, pattering presence of a small dog. I trail my fingers along the rimu join between panelling and wallpaper, wandering back to my desk and into Lady Hatwick's bedchamber...

That evening I make a platter of Brie cheese, cracked pepper wafers and local Featherston olives, and take it onto the front verandah with a Marlborough sauvignon blanc. Dusk is beginning to wane, the far paddocks are shrouded in gloom, and scent from the pink climbing roses on the white timber fretwork hangs heavily in the still air.

The cast iron benchseat feels cold but I kick off my sandals and lean back to watch the last flicker of sunset dissolve into night.

I have a growing sense of peace. Here, watching furred moths dance around the carriage lamps, listening to owls calling in the bush gully, I am far, far from my old Darlinghurst apartment, my old job and Jeffrey. Especially Jeffrey. I have to recall deliberately, almost with a start, that he is no longer in Darlinghurst but has gone back to London. Well, good riddance. And woe betide any poor English soul who falls in love with him.

I wonder briefly if it would be possible to brand a guy with a 'Beware, Bastard' sign on his forehead. You know, to warn other women. Why must it be the lot of each new, unsuspecting female to fall for the flowers, expensive gifts and money splashed around, the bewitching spell he weaves with sports cars, shining shoes and aftershave? I can still smell Jeffrey's aftershave and I flinch at the thought. I so want to show her that beneath that beautiful smile and chiseled jaw lies a heart so cold and jealous, an anger so poorly controlled that her confidence and joy will soon be shattered and her life will become a cage. A fragile, frightening cage. A lonely, hostile cage.

I flinch away from the memories and dig into the Brie. *Fuck it.* And I hear my mother's plaintive cry of 'Language, Katie!' from the recesses of my mind. So I reach for those memories instead. They are softer, warmer. They are filled with love. And I think that I would give anything right now to have my mum sitting beside me on the bench, reaching for her teapot to pour another cup, feeding morsels of fresh jam and scone to her trembling, ancient fox terrier under the table.

Mum. She didn't deserve the ending she got. But then I suppose most people don't. This thought makes me so melancholy that I toss back the rest of my glass and drag out my laptop. I need an ending for Lady Hatwick's adventures. Something to aim for.

Will the dashing Duke Everland leave his plain, heiress wife for her, or will Hattie go crawling back to her ancient husband and live unhappily ever after? Perhaps I could send her off to tour the Continent, merrily frittering away health and wealth chasing exotic intellectuals and foreign aristocrats in crumbling hilltop castles. I wouldn't mind doing that, I think, so Lady Hatwick would love it.

I spend the rest of my evening trawling through French real estate ads online, exploring chateaus with fifteen bedrooms, infinity pools, and enormous wine cellars beneath their polished parquet floors. When it gets too cold to stay outside in my short sleeves, I leave my empty bottle on the porch, plonk platter and laptop on the silent dining table and go to bed. Tonight, I feel like sleeping with the roses.

Dick Trelaney is a solid, fair-headed powerhouse of a bloke who hurtles up in his truck at eight the next morning, hauls out a hedge-trimmer and starts whipping the garden into shape before I even manage to wave hello.

The roar of motors and swift slashing of blades is brutal and overwhelming after the slow, quiet mornings I've had. He has a kid helping him, a mini-me with square shoulders and a flash of fair hair, and I remember that it's the January school holidays.

I can't hear myself think with all that noise, so I close my laptop and take my coffee onto the side verandah to watch them work.

Trelaney – I can't come at the name Dick – works fast but is gentle with the roses. "They're delicate ladies, these old plants," he says to me with a wink. "There've been roses here at Waiata Homestead for a hundred years. Gotta treat 'em like a new lover."

I want to ask him what he means, in the name of research and all that, but his boy is within earshot so I refrain. Trelaney's biceps are glistening and his hair tousled with sweat by the time they finish cutting everything back. The garden looks shocked but tidier. Better loved, somehow.

I feel my mood lift at this thought.

He sets the boy to gathering the loose branches and cuttings and stowing them in his trailer, so I come down from the verandah to help. It is pleasant work, gathering armfuls of trimmings. I breathe in the bright scent of leaves and the perfumed undercurrent of roses as I tidy and stow, and return again for more. The rose trimmings have sharp thorns, so Trelaney lends me a pair of thick gloves before we move them.

The magnolia tree on the central lawn has an uneven flourish of glossy, russet-backed new growth, so Trelaney gives it a deft haircut before he leaves. He is decisive, works fast and is kind to his son.

Later, I ask my sister Lorien about him. We are sitting in her toy-strewn lounge room, watching her boys dragging each other about in a tyre outside on the lawn.

"Dick Trelaney?" she says. "I'd forgotten about him. I should've asked him to tidy the homestead garden before you moved in." Lori tosses her ponytail with a hectic grimace.

"It's fine, he's fixed it now. Not a leaf out of place," I grin.

"He's good like that." She relaxes. "Reliable. Sometimes his boy, Logan, comes to play with my boys. They're a really nice whanau. His wife works for old man Rowan as a shepherd, while Dick does odd jobs and minds Logan."

"A shepherd? Truly? I didn't know they still existed."

Lori laughs. "Of course they do! Sheep still get lost or hurt, still need bringing down off the hills for shearing or tupping and stuff. The Rowan farm is huge, and mostly steep hill country. Nessa runs a bunch of dogs to help her."

"And of course, New Zealand has plenty of sheep," I tease, reaching for my mug of coffee. "I like the name Nessa. Maybe I can use it."

Lori's eyes brighten and she leans forward. "Speaking of which, how is your novel going?"

I frown. "I keep getting distracted. I spent most of last night looking at villas in France! But I'm enjoying the process of writing. It's just taken me a while to settle into it after moving here and after, well, you know..."

"I know." Lori exchanges a brief, sympathetic glance with me. "Such a bastard. Hang on a minute." She jumps up from the couch and leans out a window. "Boys! Leave the dog alone. She doesn't want a ride in the tyre. How about you take some cake to Olive at her house? You can all have a piece, too."

Lori shovels large slabs of cinnamon teacake into the boys' grubby hands, and wraps a few extra slices for Olive, who lives in a tiny house in the olive orchard. "Don't run while you're eating, just walk," she orders, but they run off, the eldest boy waving his plastered wrist in the air, the twins yelling like banshees.

Lori drops back onto the couch. "There, that should buy us fifteen minutes of peace." She leans forward eagerly. "So, how is the lovely Lady Hatwick getting on?"

I sigh. "Oh, she is torn. She's not sure if Duke Everland will come again. He has the title but his wife has all the money so he's not likely to leave her, no matter how ghastly their marriage is. Or how desirable Lady Hatwick is!"

"Poor Hattie. She must be so confused." Lori widens her eyes. "I think she needs a hot neighbour to distract her."

I laugh. "Doesn't everyone?" I think instantly of Lincoln, and skip quickly back to the early 1800's. "Well, she's staying with her friend, the Duchess of Devonshire, who is a remarkable woman. Historically accurate, actually. She lived openly with her husband and his lover, raised both legitimate and illegitimate children, and got involved in politics – all amazing stuff for her time. So, maybe the Duchess will have a handsome brother for our Lady Hatwick?"

"Or a coachman?" Lorien suggests, salaciously, "They could meet over a pair of steaming hot carriage horses. He could take her out every day for... riding lessons..." She wiggles her eyebrows.

"Lori," I laugh, "you should be writing this book, not me! It'd be a bodice-ripping bestseller. I'll just mind your three boys and bake teacakes and run your transport business, you know... How hard can it be?"

"I dunno. Maybe when Gus gets home from his run to Northland he could tell you?" Lori is still smiling but there's a slight edge to her tone, and I reach for her hand. I know she works hard. With Gus away so much, and with three young children at home, her life is busier than I can imagine.

I squeeze her fingers and get up. "How about I make you another drink, and you chill while I wash the dishes?" I grab our mugs from the coffee table.

"Daahling, marry me!" Lorien says, with a glorious swish of her hair. I laugh and head straight for the kitchen.

That evening, dinner with the boys is a chaotic affair. Afterwards I help Lori put them through their bath, book, bedtime routine. Nikau and Taika are hilarious together and spend most of our story-time hurtling round the bedroom, wearing their underpants on their heads. They do an endless circuit of the room, zipping past the armchair where elder brother Tommo and I sit, jumping onto the top bunk, galloping across it and leaping back down again.

I can't imagine they are able to listen to the story, tearing about like that, so I deliberately stop reading mid-sentence, and wait. The book is *Hairy Maclary from Donaldson's Dairy*, their firm favourite. To my surprise, Taika and Nikau obligingly chant the rest of the sentence to me as they wrestle each other up the ladder and tumble onto the bunk again.

"How do they do that? So many dogs' names to remember," I wonder aloud, and Tommo rolls his eyes up at me.

"They are ning nongs," he says, with all the solemn wisdom of his eight years, and we go on reading and the twins go on leaping, and eventually Lori comes in and does a lot of yelling and everyone gets into bed.

After that, Lori says she needs to work on the business accounts so I make her a green tea with lemon, say goodnight and walk home across the orchard.

As I turn up the gravel drive to the old homestead, I listen to a morepork owl calling and the skittish sigh of the night breeze in the totaras. The ancient, remnant native trees rear dark and bulky overhead and march away to my left across the Hundred Acre paddock to the river flats. Lori's house lies behind me, located on the same property but closer to the main road, with a wide circular driveway for their big trucks to turn in and a fancy new letterbox. It is not a big house, but modern and warm, and she thinks it's a better place than the old homestead to raise children in.

My new-old timber home lies ahead, sprawling and drafty, nestled within its established garden. The totara trees stand guard along the drive, the row of pines murmurs on the far side, and a bunch of decrepit outbuildings and yards lie scattered behind. I haven't explored the outbuildings properly yet, and I make a mental note to do that soon.

On the covered verandahs to the north and west, I can see roses entwined among the fretwork and forming a delicate edging around the lawns. Their leaves glitter and quiver in the moonlight and the pale flowers of the central magnolia tree seem to glow.

I pass through the garden gate and follow a path of chipped pavers to the back door. In the moonlight, I can faintly read the name 'Waiata' carved into the gate arch. The timber is mossy and old, but the gate is well-made. I sense the pride taken in the original workmanship and feel a pang of sorrow for this faded old beauty.

The back door is unlocked, as are all doors on the farm. As I step inside the house, its friendly silence settles around me like a cloak. Moonlight is streaming in through the bay windows of the front lounge. The lights of my laptop blink to my left, like a lure, in the dining room I use as an office. I turn instead into the kitchen, make a hot chocolate drink by moonlight and take this to bed in Lavender.

I don't feel like writing tonight. My head is full of the random hilarity and warm hugs of Lori's three boys, her hectic home full of noise, work and love, and my solitary walk home to this shadowy, sighing house. For the first time in weeks I feel washed up, redundant, unsure of myself. Perhaps old.

Am I old, at forty? Am I washed up? I think of Lori and all she's achieved. She is eight years younger than me. I don't regret leaving Jeffrey – I *won't* regret leaving Jeffrey – but should I have stayed in Sydney where I had colleagues, a job, a career? Should I have gone back to London? I wonder if it was madness to throw it all in and come out to Lori's farm to finish my novel. All the way across the Tasman. Most people, I tell myself, take a two-week writing retreat in the Blue Mountains and think that is enough.

They think themselves lucky, Kate. Then again, most people I know have families, homes, and other anchors to keep them in place.

Feeling fragmented and dissatisfied, I lie in bed and stare at the ceiling until I fall asleep.

Chapter 3

In the morning, I wake up with the birds and step straight outside onto the back porch and into my gumboots. Plain black with a red band around the top, they are Lori's but they fit well enough and are still cold from the night air. I am feeling a hangover of dissatisfaction from last night, a lingering restlessness, and I decide to walk it off before breakfast.

Instead of passing through the Waiata gate onto the driveway, I head out across the back garden. There, I find bare gate posts leading into a small orchard. The fruit trees are gnarled and old here, waist deep in grass and thistles. Some are still producing, however. I recognise several varieties of plums and apples, a pear, and what is perhaps a quince.

On the other side of the small orchard is the sprawl of outbuildings that were once the heartbeat of this farm. Wading through thick, knee-high grass – *calm your nerves, Katie, there are no snakes in New Zealand* – I duck under some stock rails and begin to explore.

The largest building is a compact, weatherboard barn with faded red paint, high enough to have a hay loft. There is a small hatchway above, and a rickety pulley system once used to haul feed up there. I sift through the wreckage on the ground and decide that it must once have been a stable. There are hitching rings in the heaviest posts, a few fallen rails, the remnants of cracked old leather harness in the debris on the dirt floor.

I stand for a few minutes in the cool interior, the morning light slanting around me and spiralling with dust motes. I imagine a couple of huge draught horses stamping here as they are fed and harnessed for work, and there is something in the image which calls to me.

I make my way out the back and find steel milking bails and a cement floor, indicating more recent usage of the adjacent lean-to as a dairy. There is a stone outhouse nearby with cool, stone benches and a sink, perhaps for storing milk churns and making butter and cheese. Several other sheds contain remnant feed sacks, rusted ploughs and sagging tractors.

I sit on a tractor saddle, with its stamped metalwork and flaking paint, and watch the farm wake up around me. As the tuis flit through the orchard and fantails flutter between the old sheds to catch insects on the wing, I get to dreaming about Lady Hatwick's coachman.

Would he be a gallant? A womaniser? No, I decide, he would be a practical person, salt of the earth, a rugged, quiet type. He would be older than her, competent and experienced, expert at driving large teams of high-stepping horses, maintaining carriages and managing staff. Their connection would be instant, odd, a surprise to them both. And dangerous too, so it would need to be kept secret.

I think about how to write him, and I realise that the men in my life since adulthood have been anything *but* practical, salt of the earth, quiet or rugged. They have been extroverted, flashy, wealthy and urban. Me, too. What do I know about being practical?

My father knew. I catch fleeting memories of him coming in from our garage with greasy hands after fixing our old car, of my mum laughing as he grappled with a burst pipe in the garden, of the little bookshelf he built for my fifth birthday. The last birthday he was with us, I recall, before his tumultuous relationship with Mum exploded and he fled home to New Zealand, later to meet Lori's mum and start a new life... These memories are painful and I shy away, getting back to more immediate problems.

How to write my coachman? I feel I will have to understand him, to know some of what he knows, some of what it is to drive a horse in harness, run a stable, fix carriage breakdowns and other things. Some of this I can get from internet research but I feel that would be lacking veracity somehow, truth, depth.

I step back inside the red weatherboard stable and begin to sift through the old leather on the floor. There are large brass rings, decorations, old bits and buckles and I don't know where to start. I am thinking about those horses again, the historical clop and shift of heavy, warm animals in this creaky old barn, when there is a real clop outside and a horse looms up against the broken boards of the wall.

Startled, I jump to my feet.

"Bloody hell!" Linc grabs a fistful of rein as his horse leaps sideways, as shocked as me.

I step back two paces and fall straight through a rotten timber hatch into a hole in the ground.

I hit the bottom with a thump. I lie there a moment, catching my breath. *Blimey.* I can't see a thing down here. It smells cool and earthy, like a long-undisturbed cave.

"Kate, are you alright?"

I've heard those words from Linc before. I groan and roll onto my back. Must I always appear so hopeless around him? I realise I'm still wearing the baggy shirt I slept in, a pair of tiny shorts, and Lori's gumboots.

And now I'm in a hole.

I consider my aching body. My right hip and arm are a bit sore, but otherwise I'm OK. I wonder if I can just lie here until he goes away, then I won't have to look into that handsome face and those beautiful eyes and feel so confused and inadequate.

"Yes," I reply on a sigh. "I'm OK." For someone in a hole.

Linc appears in my field of view. He looks down. "This must have been a cellar for the dairy next door."

"Do you think I care right now?" My tone is petulant. I try to get a grip, mentally.

Linc meets my eyes. "It's quite unusual round here. The farmers didn't normally bother with cellars. The water table is so high, a hole like this would often fill with water."

I scramble to my feet. "It feels dry. Do you think it could flood?" I circle, worried I'll see the walls collapse and a deluge pour in.

Linc laughs. "It's the middle of summer and it hasn't rained for days, I reckon you're safe." He reaches down with a strong, brown hand. "Want a lift out?"

"No." It's a knee-jerk reaction, but I can't bring myself to take his hand. Call it trust issues if you will. And it feels so pathetic to be rescued like that. *Kate, you're useless. And dumb to fall in, in the first place.*

Linc hesitates, and his gaze is thoughtful. I cast about for something to climb up on. A box? A pile of timber? Surely there is something down here. I will rescue myself!

There's nothing.

Linc walks away and my heart jumps to my mouth at the sound of his receding footsteps, the muffled clop of hooves. *Is he leaving? Would he do that?* I realise I don't know much at all about this man. What if I starve to death here, or drown?

I am staring up at the circle of daylight, every nerve stretched taut, when he calls out, "Watch below," and a coil of rope snakes into the hole.

"Oh." An ingenious and practical solution.

"What, did you think I would leave you here?" Linc is in view again.

"Of course not. Maybe. Who knows?" I am flustered, embarrassed, sore and cross.

Linc looks amused. "Come on, grab the rope."

"I hate being rescued by you."

His smile widens. "By me specifically, or anyone?"

"Anyone. Everyone. Oh, I don't know." This is not how my fortifying walk on the farm this morning was supposed to pan out. So much for my calm, creative life in my writer's retreat.

"Then consider it a rescue by horse. Dash is going to pull you out." He steps out of view and the rope loops and wriggles as he secures it to the saddle. I put a tentative hand on the thick, rough fibres swinging past my face.

"Ready?"

You're so useless, the voice in my head says. I take a deep breath, "Yes." *I am* not *useless.*

That's true, Katie, you are wonderful and you can do anything!

I take a strong hold of the rope and my mother's confidence, and Linc clicks to his horse. She pulls and I scramble, and in seconds I am kneeling at the top of the hole, my knees scuffed and my hands dirty, but thankfully on firm ground again.

Linc crouches down to look into my face. His tone is gentle but serious. "I would not have left you there, Kate."

I stare at him. I don't know why he needs to tell me that, or why I really, really needed to hear it. My heart is full and I don't answer, but his horse rolls her eyes at me and whickers.

Linc chuckles. "I reckon Dash thought you were a ghost. Then you crashed through the floor and gave her an even worse fright!" His horse breathes a long sigh as if to say, 'That was stressful,' and I decide I have to agree with her.

I haven't met Linc's horse before, only seen her from afar, so I reach out now and stroke her glossy neck. A childhood spent reading horsey books informs me her red-brown coat is known as 'chestnut'. I admire its glow in the morning sunshine slanting through the shed. Then I realise I've only met Lincoln twice – the day I walked under his truck, and the day he turned up at my house – and now I'm falling into holes and getting up close and personal with his horse.

I step back, feeling awkward. "Thankyou. Both of you. And I *was* actually thinking about ghosts, earlier. Before the hole." Linc raises an eyebrow and I rush on with, "Well, about the horses who must have lived here once. In this stable. And worked on the farm."

"Oh yeah." Linc's brow uncreases. "Waiata is one of the original, big farms in this district. There are old photos in town of draught horse teams ploughing these fields. And the locals sent horses down to Trentham for the troops in World War I."

"I read something about that!" I feel a flare of excitement. I love history, especially history with horses in it. "Trentham was a sort of staging camp in the Hutt Valley, where they gathered horses and troops to train them before they headed to Egypt, or somewhere..." It occurs to me my knowledge is limited – I will need to read up – but Linc doesn't seem to notice. He is hauling loose timber boards across the floor to cover the gaping hole.

"I think the horses from Waiata were mostly heavy types, Clydesdale crosses, good for pulling wagons and guns. But a lot of horses went to war from around here." He glances at his horse. "It's a shame none of them came back."

I absorb this horror for a moment, while the horse beside me rattles her bridle and breathes in and out, warm and so very much alive. I think about all those lost horses, and decide that I must do justice to the coach horses in my novel. They must come alive on the page.

"Anyway," says Linc, "I dropped by to see how your garden looks, after Dick had a go at it."

"It looks amazing," I breathe, lighting up again. I realise I have an attachment to this place already, with its ghost-filled sheds and rambling, flower-filled gardens.

Linc grins at me and I turn away, embarrassed. I wonder how I look, all covered in dirt from my adventure in the cellar. *That was so stupid, Kate.* I walk ahead and call, "Come and see, if you like."

"I will," he says airily, as though it had always been his intention, and I hide my grin as I walk. I decide, on balance, I like having him here. I'd felt this morning like I needed a distraction after my deeply introspective night, and I've certainly had one of those. And my coachman is still forming, a character in development, not yet ready for me to write.

Linc loosens the girth on Dash's saddle and walks beside me through the orchard. The long grass brushes my legs and the sun warms my face. We talk about his horse, which he named for her quick heels and turn of speed while herding cattle. She is part quarter horse – the stocky, Western horse of American cowboy fame – and part stationbred, a hardy, hillbred Kiwi mix.

"She's a good horse," he says, with a note of pride. "Easy from the beginning. She wants to help, you know? Wants to work."

"Are all quarter horses and stationbreds like that?" I'm thinking there's a lot I don't remember about horse breeds.

"Not all. Depends on their parentage, temperament, training, and experiences... They are easier to work with if everything has gone well, more difficult or nervous if they've had poor socialising. Or a traumatic experience." He glances at me. "Horses are a lot like people, really." He's smiling in his open and friendly way, but I can't help wondering if Lori has told him about Jeffrey and me.

We cross the path and walk round the corner of the house onto the central lawn. The sunlight is shining on the dew-laden grass and the roses, and there is a fantail flitting above, catching insects on the wing. The entire garden seems to sparkle and I pause to enjoy the sight.

"Sometimes, it's so beautiful I feel there could be fairies here," I breathe – but then I realise it's an odd thought and I've said it aloud. *Ghosts, falling in holes, and now fairies. Well done, Kate.*

Linc tips his head sideways. "I've often thought that." There is a wicked flash to his grin and I know he is laughing at me.

I hold his eyes and his wide smile for a moment, and feel the bubble of my own laughter rising in response. He is not judging me, I realise, and I am surprised. I think he is just laughing at my fancy, perhaps even laughing with me. I wonder if I can trust him.

We stand there on the glistening lawn, grinning at each other.

In the distant part of my brain which is still working, I recall how I was once overcome by the beauty of a simple moment and said a similar thing to Jeffrey. He made fun of my ideas then, calling me stupid, and as usual I retreated, embarrassed. But right now I feel a little older, more comfortable in this fanciful skin I own. I won't apologise, and it doesn't look like Linc expects me to.

"The garden looks good," Linc says at last, but he is still looking at me and I can't take my eyes off him. He has brown eyes. Dark like chocolate, as I have noticed before. Dark like his hair. I want to touch it, to touch *him*, and the feeling sends a flutter through me. Oh, I haven't felt like this for such a long, long...

Linc's horse nudges him, and we both react. It seems even Linc had forgotten she was there.

My defensiveness kicks in. *I don't need a man. And especially not this one, he's way too cute.* I take a quick step back and look away.

Linc clears his throat. "Righto. I've got two horses to pick up from Fletcher's place, so I'll head off now. Please promise not to fall into any more holes."

I open the garden tap and begin scrubbing my hands clean. "I promise. No more holes."

"Good-oh." He swings into the saddle.

I wave him on his way, then walk through the French doors into my still, silent house. I sit down at my desk and experience a complete blank. I can't recall what I'm supposed to be writing or doing. I can think only of that long-legged, chestnut horse and her rider, striding away down the drive.

At last I get up, slip out of my grubby clothes and toss them in the basket in the bathroom. I stand under a hot shower until my grazes stop stinging and my hair feels clean again. Then I dry off, dress in fresh shorts and a sweatshirt and head back to my office.

The coachman, my memory prompts me at last. I reach for the keyboard. I recall Linc's tanned arms beneath rolled sleeves, his strong, quick hands and light, easy smile – and I know now how my coachman looks. Perhaps about ten years older, and dressed in livery. Their first introduction 'over a pair of steaming hot carriage horses', as Lori suggested, comes easily enough, and I enjoy a rapid flow of words until I realise I'm a bit hazy on what Hattie's love interest would wear when driving his coach. And that's important when you are trying to write his kit off him. I search online and find a goldmine of historical websites.

I spend the next hour utterly absorbed in descriptions of the clothing, manners and duties prescribed for Regency era coachmen and grooms. I also research the valet, cook, and other domestic servants. The glaring distinctions of class and wealth between servant and master are not lost on me as I read, but I gain a new understanding of the way these classes were intertwined, each dependent on the other for assistance and reputation as individuals sought to climb the social ladder. I see that so many were vulnerable, ripe for exploitation.

I realise there are numerous places in my manuscript where I could use this detail, so I spend the rest of my day happily fitting it in wherever it works.

Tonight I sleep in Bluebell, tracing the delicate wallpaper flowers with screen-bright eyes until I finally drift off.

Linc rides Dash home on a loose rein, gazing ahead but paying little attention. The horse knows her way home anyway, and he's got something else to think about. A something with pale skin and shining hair and worried, green eyes he could drown in. A something dressed in tiny shorts and an oversized shirt, rounded in all the right places.

He groans. He so wanted to kiss off those smudges and run his fingers under that shirt, yet she wouldn't even take his hand so he could save her.

"Get up, Dash," he says, and they canter home over the Hundred Acre paddock. Sue will be at the homestead. She'll help set his mind straight.

Chapter 4

It appears my mornings are destined to be disturbed this week. I've barely got my feet onto the floorboards at dawn and a coffee in my hand, before there is an almighty cacophony of barking and yelling outside on my driveway. It sounds like a cataclysmic argument between a bunch of banshees and the hounds of hell, and it is coming towards me.

I step outside in trepidation, and something I have never seen before appears between the totara trees.

First, the dogs arrive. There are four of them. They are enormous, hairy and wolf-like, with wide open, slathering jaws. They are running and barking, barking and running, with the occasional snap and a yelp. They are harnessed to a sled which they are dragging along, hauling up the road, and they look like they're enjoying themselves hugely.

Inside this flurry of noisy mayhem is a woman. She is riding on the sled, her spiky silver hair standing out from her head like a halo, yodelling at the dogs as she urges them along. And after the sled come Lori's three boys, pedalling their bicycles madly in pursuit, shouting and laughing and having as much fun as the dogs.

The melee sweeps past the homestead and envelopes me in its noise. The woman catches my eye and grins and waves, all the while clutching grimly to the sled. The dogs barely give me a glance as they tear past the Waiata gate, still barking and running, and hurtle on up the farm track between the sheds.

Tommo skids to a stop. "Hello, auntie Kate!" His face is glowing, and he is panting with the exertion of chasing this dog-powered contraption across the farm.

"Tommo, what on earth...?" I am laughing and incredulous.

"We're taking the dogs for a run with Olive."

"Oh, is that Olive? You know, most people take their little dogs for a run in the park..."

"We running da nuskies!" It is Nikau, screeching to a stop and causing a small bicycle pileup with Taika behind him.

"Huskies, you idiot," corrects Tommo.

"Nuskies are running!" agrees Taika, climbing out of the wreckage. He clouts his brother, they disentangle their bikes, then both twins shout, "Bye!" and hurtle off again in hot pursuit.

Tommo rolls his eyes and I smile in sympathy. He says seriously, "I need to go with them. Last time, they tried to overtake the dogs and Maple didn't like it."

"Maple?"

"The lead dog!" Tommo calls over his shoulder as he pedals away.

Oh. I'm impressed that Lori's boys still have all their limbs and organs if Maple had taken offence.

I stand on my verandah, listening to the little cyclone of barking and yelling fade into the distance as it progresses across the farm. Around me, birdsong starts up again and a few brave, birdy souls flit out of hiding to resume their morning's work, foraging for food and singing their territories.

Huskies. That's new.

They're lovely, Katie, but I prefer my Foxy.

Olive turns up again to meet me in person, later that afternoon. She is minus the dogs this time but driving a little green car which she navigates with haphazard glee, bumping over a rose bush and parking in the middle of my lawn.

"Oops, sorry about your Belle de Crecy. Hello, how are you Kate, I've heard all about you, I'm Olive." She tumbles out of her car and strides over to shake my hand. Olive is tall, slender, perhaps in her sixties, with a shock of silver hair to match her nonstop energy.

I manage to say hello amid the stream of conversation, and offer coffee. Soon we are perched around the wrought iron table on the front porch. Olive is talking energetically about her huskies and I am listening and laughing, when she pauses for a moment and studies me over the rim of her cup.

She nods. "Oh yes, I can see why he's interested." And I am not sure if she is referring to me or the coffee. *Who is interested? In what?* "Tell me, Kate, what are your plans while you are here? Do you want a job?"

"Pardon?"

"A job," Olive grins. "Commonly performed for monetary gain but studiously avoided by a small portion of the population. Do you want one?"

"Oh. I hadn't thought about it. I'm here to write my book, mostly. I have Mum's money to draw on, but..."

"But writing is a lonely exercise, I imagine." Olive's gaze is hawk-like.

"Well, yes." I realise now that, excepting Lori, Olive is the first guest I've invited into my new-old house for coffee. My circle of acquaintances here is very small. "I suppose I could do with more reasons to get out of the house."

"You certainly could. You don't even have a dog. My dogs get me out of the house every day. What do you think, Kate, would you like a dog?"

I laugh. "How about I start with a job first?"

"Excellent." Olive has finished her coffee so she stands up. "I can offer you one starting tomorrow. Please say yes, I need help now and then in my bookstore, most often serving coffee and sometimes selling books. It will only be part-time, but it's in the middle of town, I promise you it will be fun."

I surprise myself by saying, without hesitation, "It sounds perfect."

What's this, Katie? You are being spontaneous!

"Wonderful, I'll pick you up in the morning. Lovely to meet you, Kate, you are all that Lori promised, and himself too, thanks for the coffee. One day I'll introduce you to my dogs, you're going to love them." Then with a bump and a skid, Olive is gone.

I shake my head and escape back into my Regency world.

Early next morning, I hear the roar of a little engine outside, the scatter of gravel and a toot-toot. I look outside and see Olive waving at me from her car window. I am awake but only just, half-comatose and nursing my first coffee, watching birds through the big bay window of my loungeroom.

I remember with a shock that I promised Olive I'd be her barista, helping in her bookshop in Mayton. I sprint barefoot into the kitchen, pour my coffee into a travel mug, then run down the hall to my big wardrobe in the Rose room. I haul on linen pants, a close-fitting floral tee and light linen jacket. I grab my wallet and drag on my Doc Martens, slam the back door behind me and slip into the passenger side of Olive's car.

"Good morning!" Olive sings out. "You forgot, didn't you." It's a statement not a question, and she is smiling.

"Never," I say. "Absolutely not. Who are you again?" And I grin, and she laughs, and we are soon hurtling down the drive in her little green hatchback and out onto the road. Olive's frizzhaired, raucous energy is infectious and I decide I like her.

Mayton is picture perfect this morning. The long row of white-painted timber storefronts are aglow in the slanting, first rays from the sun and a light mist drifts up through the treetops. The fields around town are glittering with dew, and a few people are stirring here and there – opening shop doors, warming their car engines, walking up the street for coffees.

I feel glad now that Olive has rushed me out of my cold, quiet house and into a busy day of new scenes and company.

Olive's Little Bird Bookshop is tucked under a verandah, in a three-sided courtyard facing the main street. The paved expanse contains several ornate benches and a flagpole. At first, I can't imagine anyone actually uses the courtyard, but I am proved wrong because when Olive parks out the back, unlocks her shop, and fires up the coffee machine, it is like a magnet to the locals. Next door is a wool fashion brand, on the other side is a real estate agency, and over the road lie two antique stores, an art gallery and a rural livestock feed store. Before long, everyone shows up.

Our customers arrive at the wide, open coffee window in twos or threes, chatty and friendly. They form a trickle light enough that I can keep up with the orders, but steady enough that by eleven I am feeling my feet. I meet Daisy, the self-confessed cat lady, and dubious old Vaughan, and late thirties Brad from the real estate agency, who leans a little too close and smiles with all his teeth at me. I had forgotten what it was like standing in front of a coffee machine all day, greeting customers, asking for their order, making smalltalk. I feel exhausted. It has been a while, after all.

I take advantage of a lull to sit on a stool beside the machine and daydream a little. I realise I haven't worked as a barista since before I met Jeffrey. In fact, that was *how* I met Jeffrey. That is not a rewarding line of thought, so I look around for Olive.

After initially checking that I was confident with the coffee production part of her business, Olive has been in her little office all morning. She pops her head out now and asks, "Have you had enough barista-ing yet?"

"Yes, I am thinking of tendering my resignation and running away to Peru."

"Well, you can't," Olive says delightedly, "you don't even officially work here yet so resignation is not an option. Peru might be, but then you'd have to take me with you. I've always wanted to go to Peru."

"That sounds like a plan. I'll tell Lori I'm leaving tomorrow."

"Oh no, don't," laughs Olive. "Her boys will want to come too, and then our trip will get crowded."

"Ohhh…" I roll my eyes. "Imagine!"

"Yes." Olive contemplates the idea for a moment. "Although, if we could keep Taika and Nikau from causing an international incident, I think they'd be great to have along. And Tommo would pick up Spanish or Quechua in a heartbeat."

"Yes, he's a bright lad, that one."

"Like his auntie." Olive's sun-lined face is smiling kindly.

I feel myself blushing. "I don't know. I think Lori is the smarter one of us. She's got her life way more organised than mine could ever be."

"You have a lot of heart, Kate, don't underestimate yourself."

And I look at Olive and I think, this is what conversations with her are like. They start off light and humorous, but then within a blink she is discussing world peace or South-east Asian politics or the complexity of your heart. Or dogs. Because Olive must have read my discomfort and she heads off now on a story about the years she has spent keeping husky dogs, and how one of her original females was the alpha but had a heart as big as an elephant's, "an incredible animal, I will never forget her."

"I meant to ask about your dogs," I say. "Aren't huskies, you know, just one step removed from a wolf? Lots of sharp teeth and hunting instincts, that sort of thing?"

Olive laughs. "They are natural hunters and killers, yes, so you have to keep them away from small animals. But they love people, just *love* them. After keeping huskies I could never have any other dog. You're right, though, they need excellent training and lots of exercise, lots and lots. And you've got to stay the boss of them, you can't let them start to boss you." She looks at me contemplatively for a moment and adds, "Kate, don't take this the wrong way but please don't ever get a husky."

"I promise." I cross my heart. "To be honest, the thought has never crossed my mind. But what about the sled? Do they like pulling it, and running like that?"

"Oh yes," says Olive, as if having sled dogs is the most natural thing in the world. "I train all my dogs to pull, we go sled racing on the South Island. It's great fun."

I stare at her in awe. "That's amazing."

"Olive can train anything," says a familiar voice over my left shoulder. I spin to make eye contact.

Linc.

He is grinning at us. "She helps me with the horses sometimes, and she always works wonders. Don't stand still too long, Kate, or she'll train you. Actually, seeing as you're here, she probably has!"

"She may be well trained but she's not working very hard," Olive scolds. I jump to attention as she gives me a friendly wink and disappears back into her office.

I am left with Linc.

He looks fresh and warm and way more energetic than I feel, and I unaccountably want to climb over the counter and kiss him. Instead, I tuck away a stray lock of ponytail and say, "Coffee?"

He asks for a long black. I am so flustered I almost put milk in it, and he notices.

"I reckon I oughta tell Olive to repeat the training around black coffees, that's not quite locked in yet." His voice is rich and warm, like his smile.

"Don't you dare. It's just that most of the orders this morning have been flat whites. And you interrupted *my* coffee break, so you get the second-rate service."

"Olive!" he calls. "She's giving me second-rate service out here!"

"I always knew you deserved it, Lincoln Brady," is Olive's breezy reply.

He shrugs. "I dunno. You just can't get quality staff these days."

"Not here in Little Bird, anyway," I smile. "If you go further up the road, you may find fabulous coffee."

"This will do," says Linc, taking his coffee and a seat at the window in one smooth movement. And I wonder if that statement means he is settling for second best or if he really wants to stay, then I admonish myself for reading way too much into one short sentence and get super busy cleaning the coffee machine.

When I look up again, Linc is reading the community newspaper on the counter and I get a good look at his amazing profile, framed by sunlight in the courtyard behind him. I find I want to know everything about him. Everything. From how he felt on his first day at school, to what he had for breakfast this morning and which brand of toothpaste he likes.

This urge is so sudden, strong and startling that I reach for the small things I do know about him and start there. "Did you collect the horses OK yesterday?"

He looks up distractedly. "Yeah, they loaded in the truck alright. I put the grey through the round pen this morning and he was sweet, did everything textbook."

"There are textbooks for horses in round pens?"

"Of course." He is laughing at me again, with that telltale crinkle in his eyes. "Nah, he just did exactly what a horse is supposed to do when I start the round pen work. He moved away when I asked, he dropped his head a minute or two after I moved him on, he came in when I stepped back. The whole shebang."

"Ohhh," and it is Olive, leaping into the conversation now with her trademark enthusiasm. "He joined up perfectly then! Did he lick and chew? Was he listening to you?"

"He had his ear on me straight away. I tell you, Olive, he's a gem. You don't want a horse, do you? This one is a cracker." And they are away, speaking a different language to any I know, comparing round pen techniques and horses they've trained.

I let their conversation wash comfortably round me as I prepare a large lunchtime coffee order for the staff of the real estate office across the court. A perfectly toned, skirt-suited, brunette powerhouse called Christa soon comes to collect them, and I engage in enough smalltalk with her to be left feeling completely inadequate and frumpy by the time her coffees are ready.

It seems that Linc has hardly noticed Christa, he is so engaged in talking with Olive about horses, but her eyes rest on him far longer than necessary as she scoops up her tray of hot drinks.

I know, I think, *he's gorgeous. Now please go back to your office and flirt with up-and-coming Brad from the next desk instead, with his shiny new Audi and fledgling investment portfolio. This one likes horses. Those heels of yours will skid in his stable muck.*

Christa strides away across the flagstones, and I polish the chromework on the coffee machine madly while I growl, *Bloody hell*, under my breath, and wish I were less jealous, less short, less round and generally less flawed, let's be honest.

"You'll dissolve the metalwork if you keep going like that... Um, Kate?" And I look up to realise Olive has gone back to her office, and Linc is addressing me.

"What?" His gaze is uncertain and I wonder if I've been abrupt or weird, then figure I've probably been both. "Sorry. I was thinking."

"Do you do that often? Because the chrome on Olive's coffee machine may not survive it."

I relax a little because his crinkly eyes are back and he's looking at me like I'm some kind of odd but amusing exhibit. "I'll try to reform. Honest. No more thinking for the rest of the day."

"Primo. You're in Mayton now, Kate, not Oxford or inner-city London. Dumb it down or you'll put us all to shame." He slides his long legs off the counter stool and gives me a nod. "I'm off to help Gilford with some lambs, I'll see you round."

Yes, very round. "Bye." And I watch him walk over to his ute and wonder if I've always been obsessed with my weight and my weirdness, or if this is Jeffrey's voice I am hearing in my head, not mine. I don't know. My life prior to Jeffrey seems to blur into the life I led with him.

All I can be sure of is that it's not my mother's voice. She was as round as me and never seemed to care, dressing just as she liked and telling me I was perfect as I was.

Oh, Mum.

And the next few hours until Olive closes the bookshop seem like some of the longest in my life. I feel a deep, deep exhaustion and sadness and it takes all of my hard-learned social skills to be polite to the customers and chatty with Olive.

Olive's conversation on the way home distracts me, but when I am alone in my old house I kick off my shoes, lie on the couch to rest my feet, and my thoughts come crowding back.

Why am I feeling like this? I try to pinpoint the cause. But all I can imagine is that I miss my mum and I feel inadequate after meeting powerhouse Christa from the estate agency, and that all seems ridiculous at the age of forty.

Seriously, Katie.

It doesn't stop me from curling up round a couch cushion, leaking a few tears and drifting into an exhausted sleep before it is even dark outside.

Chapter 5

I wake very early in the morning with a crick in my neck and freezing cold feet. The house has cooled down overnight, and I patter across the rickety boards to drag a blanket and woolly ugg boots from my wardrobe. The sky is just beginning to lighten, so I take my blanket and a cup of breakfast tea outside to the cast iron bench.

I watch as a white mist which has settled across the front paddock overnight rises slowly with the arrival of the sun, and the grass glows gold then emerald. Across the misty paddock, in the dense stand of totara trees, a tui is singing his morning territorial round.

I decide to shake off my melancholy from yesterday and be grateful for the things I have. For Lori and my three nephews, for my writing, for this old homestead and its beautiful view. For Olive, as a new and fantastical friend, and Linc, for the feelings he is awakening in me. Surely if I feel like this I will write a better romance novel? Even if it is putting me into a tailspin and bringing back all the pain of mum's passing, my life with Jeffrey, my failures.

"That's it, Katie, use and abuse," I say aloud with a grin, and take my teacup into the kitchen. *Who said a writer's life would be an easy one?*

Olive toot-toots outside my house while I am dressing. This time I am in layered black with tan, knee-high boots and huge, brightly-coloured earrings. I feel better prepared for a day at the bookshop now I know what to expect, and Olive's chatter washes merrily over me as we hurtle into Mayton, swing past the real estate office, and pull up with a squeal behind her little, weatherboard building. I give Olive's diminutive car a pat of respect as we climb out – I don't know how it survives her ministrations. We unlock the door, fire up the coffee machine and get into our routine.

I see no Linc today, plenty of Christa, and I meet the three Carlisle sisters who run the wool fashion label next door and an antique store across the road. The two older sisters are in their early fifties, I guess, well-spoken and well-dressed in a classic, discreet, antiques collector manner. The youngest sister is louder, more outgoing, wearing a bold, black and white pant suit and bright purple hair.

"Billie," she says, sticking out her hand and shaking mine, "Billie Carlisle. That's Derryn there in the beige, Roma in the blue. They'll have flat whites with almond milk, no sugar, but you can make mine a mocha with two. I apologise for our names, our parents had visions of grandeur and wanted boys, perhaps. I think I was a particular disappointment to them."

She says all this with a merry tilt of her head and a laugh, and I can't help but grin in return. Billie is flamboyant, her energy irresistible. Derryn and Roma have struck up a conversation with Olive as soon as they entered, and I listen to their description of an international book fair they attended last year in Berlin, while I get onto Billie's list.

One day, that could be me. I just have to finish this flaming book. And the next three hours until Olive closes her bookshop pass easily for me, in a drift of reverie and smalltalk. I feel I am settling into the gentle rhythm of this town's comings and goings.

Making coffees is not getting my novel written, however, and I am glad that on Thursday morning Olive doesn't need me. I lie in bed as the sun rises, watching leaf shadows dancing on the ceiling of the Sunflower room, thinking about Lady Hatwick and her coachman.

When I feel like I am ready, I get up and write two thousand flawless, flowing, scorching words that launch him right off the page into her heart and her bed. The Chatsworth horses are so beautiful, she is so utterly infatuated, and he is so compelling and magnetic that I am fully absorbed and totally miss Linc's arrival at my gate.

He approaches from behind and lifts her skirt, trailing his hand up the inside of her lace-draped thigh. She tips her head back and leans against him, her rounded breasts tight-laced and heaving. He grunts approval, and probes a little higher with his fingers – she is wet, warm, ready for him.

He longs to tear her breasts free of her corset, kiss her soft skin, push her down and take his pleasure. But first, he will tease until she begs, her lips parted and her legs... His silhouette appears without warning at the open French doors, and I jump out of my skin.

"Oh, blimey!"

"Are you OK?" Linc looks concerned.

"Just lost in my story." I press a hand to my breast to soothe my galloping heart. I wonder at his sudden arrival, then realise

I'd been lost with my coachman in the voluminous depths of Lady Hatwick's petticoats. There'd been so much gasping and heavy petting going on, it had been impossible to hear him over the din.

"I had to drop something at Olive's house, so I thought I'd call in on my way back."

"Well, it's nice to see you." I realise this is in fact true, despite his interruption of the best flow of writing I've had in days. Forbidden foreplay with Regency era stable staff be damned, I think, Hattie can wait while I spend a few minutes interacting with a real, live male of the modern era. It's not like I meet many of them, after all.

Dash is there too, and Linc turns away to loop the reins over her neck. I take a moment to twirl briefly in the sun, then jump the few steps down from the verandah.

"Breakfast?" I ask, because this man is making me feel good just by being here and I want to keep him a little longer.

"Sweet," he says, and it is a word of acceptance and appreciation, like 'sure' or 'perfect'. I feel I may be getting the hang of the local dialect. I open the French doors more fully to the sunlit morning, and head in through my office-slash-dining room, noting that the air inside my house is colder than outside now, anyway.

"Eggs?" I ask, and he says yes. Then I ask, "Scrambled OK?" and he says yes again, and I decide that I should come up with some real-life sentences longer than one or two words soon. I rummage through the kitchen to find free range eggs, herbs, a whisk and a heavy skillet. He leans against the timber doorframe in a decorative fashion, like a lean, rangy horseman from a black and white western movie, but in blue jeans and without the ten-gallon hat.

I scramble the eggs, and he scrambles my thoughts just by being there, and not much intelligent gets said really until we are back out on the verandah setting the skillet on the outdoor table. I rustle up some plates and cutlery, chop and arrange fresh peppers, kiwifruit and oranges, and breakfast begins to look festive. We pull up the chairs and get comfortable. I sit with the light behind me, however, because although I might be scrambled right now, I do remember that forty-something may not look exactly stunning in bright sunlight.

Linc doesn't notice. He hands out the cutlery as if it's his home, not mine, and we dig in.

"Cheers," I say, pouring him a coffee, and he raises his cup in salute. "So," I say brightly, then I flinch because Jeffrey hated me starting conversations with 'so'. But he's not here so I go ahead with, "What's on your schedule today?"

"I thought I'd start Fletcher's bay mare. She's head shy and girthy so he asked me to do some work with her, see if she'll settle down."

"Girthy?"

"Freaks out when you tighten the saddle girth. She's more extreme than most, she lashes out and tries to bite. He reckons she pulled so hard once that she tore the tether ring out of his truck."

"Not ideal."

"No." The laugh lines around his eyes crinkle. "So, that will be fun. And tomorrow, I'm going into Wellington for the afternoon. I've gotta deliver some leatherwork to the guys at

Weta Workshop, then there's an open mike night at the Blues Club."

"I've heard of Weta, they're a famous film studio. What do you do with leather?"

"I usually fix saddles and make harness for people. Weta asked me to do some work on Lord of the Rings costumes, and the work's trickled on from there. They have their own guys, but when they want something special they give me the design and I try not to stuff it up."

"Yeah, right."

"Yeah, true. Sometimes their ideas are really *out* there."

I smile. "I suppose that comes with the artistic personality. And what about the open mike?"

"Oh, I like to drop in on them now and then. The muso scene is pretty small around Wellington, so I almost always meet someone I know there to jam with."

"What do you play?"

"Guitar. Bass. Blues harp. Depends who's already set up there."

I look at him with interest. It is definitely my urban prejudices getting in the way, but I hadn't ever imagined a horse trainer who could wrangle sheep, create intricate movie costumes and play blues music on the fly. There is a lot going on with Linc. And I had inadvertently tossed him in the 'cute local yokel neighbour' pile. Dumb.

So, I ask him a few more questions and we talk about everything from the weather to the complexities of crafting leather gauntlets for orcs, and to me it seems all too soon that he is pushing back his chair and his plate.

"Thankyou for breakfast, Kate," he says appreciatively, and I like the way he says my name. "It was a much better meal than I would have made myself." There's that flash of a grin again.

"Me too," I agree. "I cook less when I'm on my own. It's harder to make the effort, somehow." I hope that doesn't sound like some kind of hint, but the sun is warm here on the verandah and his smile is warm, and my brain is not working like it should.

His next words are unexpected. "Yeah, I eat better when Sue is home. But she's working in Auckland this week."

My stomach drops. I feel flattened. Unsure.

"Does she work in Auckland often?" I ask casually. I want to say, 'Who is Sue? Lori didn't mention any Sue!' but that would be a stretch for my polite, English upbringing. I want to scratch Sue's eyes out, even though she may have lived with him for twenty years and I've only spoken with him a few times. I realise that, while Lori didn't mention any Sue, she didn't say Linc was single either.

Kate, your imagination is running away with you again. I calm down, try to make eye contact but act a little cooler.

Linc is concentrating on stacking the plates and answers absently. "Usually she works out of Wellington, but sometimes all over the place. She's an immunologist by trade, but Chief Executive now. She delivers projects, deals with all the shareholders and stuff. The company business includes vaccine development, so she's pretty busy liaising with government ministries and whatever."

What is it with all the independent, accomplished women round here? I wonder. *What on earth happened to me?*

"She's away a lot then, that must be difficult," I say sympathetically, and Linc looks at me a little strangely, but goes on tidying.

When Linc has all the dishes in a neat pile, he takes them into the kitchen and starts running water into the sink. I don't know whether to help him with the dishes or sit and be decorative, so I settle for offering to go and check on Dash, though we can both see her through the window.

Dash is sleeping in the sunshine, one hoof hitched and her saddle girth loose. I reach one hand towards her and she breathes over it politely, heaves a long sigh, then goes back to dozing. I plait a few tendrils of her mane and enjoy her warm, horsey scent for a while.

I think about Linc and Sue. That doesn't go anywhere pleasant, so I think back instead to all the horse and pony books I read when I was a child, and the passion I'd had for horses. It had burned so fiercely. I'd had pony posters on my walls, subscriptions for pony club magazines, an eclectic model horse collection. If it had four legs, a mane, and whinnied, I was obsessed with it. My mother, a city girl born and bred, hadn't understood at all.

I wonder now where all that passion went.

The gurgle of sink water alerts me that the dishes are done, so I head back to the house. Linc meets me on the verandah and for a moment I am transfixed by the sight of him. He is standing a few steps above me, smiling quizzically at me in the bright sun, his shadow casting a lean stripe across the timber boards.

"Did you enjoy communing out here?" he asks.

I glance back at Dash. "I think she found me boring. She fell asleep."

He chuckles. "She does that to me, too. She's not really one for conversation."

"That's probably what makes her good company," I say, just to see that grin again.

Linc unties the leadrope, tightens the saddle girth and swings onto his horse. Dash pricks up her ears, flicks her tail and moves off at the slight touch of his heel. I wave, as he does, and watch him ride away down the drive.

He is Sue's, I remind myself firmly. But my overwhelming feeling is, *Blimey, that will be hard to remember.*

I spend Friday morning at the bookshop with Olive, helping her unpack a new order in between coffee-making duties. I soon find that I am reading more than I am cataloguing. I am immersed in a compelling history of the Light Horse Brigade in World War I when there is a great scuffle and shouting at the door, and Lori's boys come tumbling in.

"Auntie Kate, we saw a wubbish twuck!" Taika's eyes are huge.

"Yes, it was kyekting wubbish! A hyuge one!" Nikau nods furiously.

"*Collecting* rubbish, you nongs," says Tommo, following them sedately, lifting his plastered arm in greeting. "And it wasn't that huge. I've seen bigger." He glances at me with the pained expression of one who must live with fools, then swiftly surveys the room. "You've got new books?" he asks Olive.

"Oh yes," Olive enthuses, "including some fabulous stories based on real-life, historical letters, come and see." She takes him over to the kids' History section and they are soon deep in conversation.

I turn my attention to the younger boys. Taika has zeroed in on the coffee machine and is climbing onto a stool, promising to make his twin a 'fyat white' with 'yots' of sugar. Nikau is tearing the tops off sugar packets in preparation. I intercept a near disaster with the hot water, and am just scootching Taika's stool out of reach of the coffee machine when Lori and Gus turn up at the coffee window.

"Hello, you two," I grin. "The cavalry arrived, so I figured you must be somewhere nearby."

"Yes." Lori grimaces. "Sorry about that. We ran into Nessa outside the bank and got talking, then the boys disappeared."

Gus nods. "We followed the trail of destruction and shocked witnesses here." I look into his hazel eyes and see the crinkle of humour that infuses the fabric of his hectic, hardworking life with Lori.

Lori laughs, he wraps an arm around her and they grin at each other. I wonder if I'll ever have someone look at me with love like that. Pure, simple, unconditional love. I know Jeffrey doesn't understand what unconditional love is; he is all about transactions and control.

Lori is talking, and I drag myself back to the present.

"Nessa said she'd like some help with the flowers, so I've volunteered you and I to go round there early on the big day, just to put the finishing touches on everything, you know, the bunting, the table settings, the stage..."

"The what?" I have a feeling I've missed something. I scoop Nikau off the window bench and intercept Taika's grab for the cocoa shaker while I try to remember what she said.

"Nessa is organising her best friend's wedding," Lori explains. "It's on a Saturday, two weeks' time, at the Brady's Summer Homestead. There will still be roses then, and the pergola on the western terrace will look amazing." She barely draws breath as she adds, "Taika, let auntie Kate make the coffees. Nikau, stop swinging on the door handle or it'll fall off and you'll have to stay and be Olive's doorman for the rest of your life."

Nikau looks amused by this thought but he leaves the door handle alone, and I get on with making a mochaccino for Lori and a long black for Gus. I don't even know where the Brady's Summer Homestead is, although I've a feeling I should know something about it. Gus talks a bit about his recent trip to Northland with the truck, then Lori extracts Tommo from his conversation with Olive by buying two books and promising to bring him back next week to buy the rest.

She rolls her eyes at me and I wave them all down the street, then turn back to see Brad and Christa from Real Estate queuing up with their colleagues, and I realise it's lunchtime already.

Chapter 6

The next rush is mid-afternoon. As I tidy up, Brad lingers at the window, the sole remaining customer. When at last he finishes his soy cappuccino and wanders off, I go outside to dispose of the coffee grinds. I pause there a moment, lifting my face to the sun, enjoying the brief respite from being indoors.

Olive pokes her head round the door. "Someone inside to see you."

She has a smug look on her face. I raise my eyebrows but Olive won't say, so I go into the bookshop and Linc is there. His boots are polished and he looks dressed for town, not the farm – new, dark brown moleskins, a cream open-necked shirt that highlights the tan of his skin, his hair still wet from the shower.

"I'm heading into Wellington," he says casually. "It occurred to me you might like to get out of here, go see the Big Smoke. Do you want to come?"

"What?" I am so surprised, I stare at him. "I don't think I can. Olive needs me."

Linc looks at Olive and something indefinable passes between them. Olive grabs a teatowel from the bench and flicks it at me. "Pish, I don't need you, go and have some fun."

"What?" I say again. My mouth is on autopilot while my brain catches up and I am thinking, *I hate surprises, I'm not ready, I'm not dressed for going into the city! And what will Sue say if I go out with Linc?*

Olive is looking amused. "It's just a drive to Wellington and back. He's a good guy, Kate, he won't bite."

Linc takes a step back, perhaps sensing my panic. "Have a think about it. No pressure. I'll wait outside."

"No, I..." I feel my inherent anxiety settling in. I look down at my slim black tee and black pants and feel I am channeling my inner barista beautifully here, but am in no way ready to meet talented designers from Weta Workshop, or musicians at a blues bar. What will people say? Do I want to go? Yes! *But not now, not so... soon!*

"You should see some more of Wellington. It will be fun, Kate." Olive has her head tilted and her hands on hips.

I am still hesitating when a small, inner voice reminds me that I've missed out on cool things before because of my fears, because of my knee-jerk 'no' gene, that I should shut up and just go with it today.

I take a deep breath. "OK."

"Do you have a jacket?" Olive checks. "It might be cold in Wellington. Windy." I don't, but she tosses me that riotous, Guatemalan thing of hers that I've joked before is her Cloak of Many Colours. "Don't put it on until you're well out of sight. It will look far better on you than me, and I'd rather not see." She laughs, and we leave.

We leave. Linc and me. Together. I feel teenage-awkward to be getting in his ute with him and I'm not sure what I think about that. Excited. Nervous. Unsure what to say. Stressed. Self-conscious.

Linc's ute is a restored, blue Holden Kingswood. I put my purse and Olive's quilted jacket on the bench seat between us. Linc uses the column shift to move into first, and we pull away from the kerb. There is a satisfying rumble from the small-block V8 under the bonnet as we cruise through Mayton, and Linc opens her up a little on the straight stretch south to Featherston. He is driving with his window down and his sleeves rucked up, just like he had in the truck – one tanned elbow on the sill, the sunlight streaming in over the range from the west. The distant hills are like blue shadows in the afternoon light.

It is too noisy to talk much over the motor and the wind, so I settle back and try to relax. I like this old car, the burble of the engine, the tan leather interior and chrome trim around the dash. Like Gus's truck had reminded me of my father, this one puts me in memory of my mum and her old Bentley. She owned that car for decades, a sleek old gentleman of the road, until it was sold when she became too ill to drive. I can still picture the smooth lines and luxurious upholstery in my mind's eye.

I chuckle to think that I am comparing a splendid British car of flawless pedigree with an upstart Aussie utility vehicle, and Linc raises an eyebrow questioningly. I shake my head and he grins, and we drive on, following the blue curve of the road into Featherston. We pass the Fell Locomotive Museum, a line of trim little shops, burble over the railway line and into the foothills of the Remutaka Range.

Soon, the old Kingswood is rumbling over a bridge, hauling up the steep grade of the range, growling as Linc double-clutches into second, dipping into the first tight bend then the next. In the summer afternoon haze, the ride through corner after corner, up and over this imposing range becomes mesmerising. I roll down my window and let the wind ruffle my hair, bringing with it the scent of forested hills and cool, high altitude air.

I could be making coffees for Christa and her crew right now. I'm glad that I am not.

We emerge from the hills to pick up the broad, picturesque Hutt River, and follow it down to the harbour and around into the city. Linc's car creates an echoing rumble between the high-rise buildings and bounces off the chunky stonework of Victoria Tunnel.

Weta Workshop is nestled on a peninsula girt by water, along a wide street dotted with weatherboard villas. There, Linc rolls back a tarp on the ute tray and opens a lockbox, dragging out an armful of carved, leather strapping and polished brass buckles.

"Want to come in?" he asks. I'm feeling awkward, so I tell him that I'll walk down to look at the nearby theatre instead. He disappears inside a wide door flanked by hulking orc statues, and I wander off down the road. I'd seen the theatre on our way in, and it isn't very far. It had caught my eye because it is a splendid building in Art Deco style, and I am entranced now as I step inside.

Roxy Cinema is resplendent with decorated ceilings, ornate tiles and plasterwork and subdued lighting, which I discover is all due to a painstakingly careful restoration taken almost ten years before. As I order a pot of tea in CoCo Restaurant from the friendly and informative waiter, I settle to watch filmgoers enter and leave, children ordering ice creams, locals passing by the front windows. The street is giving me a relaxed, summer vibe.

I get to thinking about how quiet my life is, on Lori's farm. It is so different from my life in Sydney with Jeffrey, so removed from my previously urban existence and everything I've known, that I feel almost dislocated. Different.

Better?

I'm not sure. I think so. Definitely better without Jeffrey. I cannot imagine why I am thinking about him again today but perhaps it is the busyness of the cars outside, the luxury of this building. Jeffrey is all about luxury, money, ostentatious wealth. All about power.

I flinch reflexively, and Linc's voice is there to anchor me as he says, "Bad dream?"

I haul myself back to the present. His boots have made no sound on the thickpile carpet and I don't know how long he's been watching me.

"Yes. No," I stumble. "Just something best left in the past." I am somehow unable to lie to him.

I wait for a cross-examination but Linc just studies my face for a moment then reaches out to me. "Come," he says.

I don't take his hand but I follow him out of the cinema and down the street to his car. Linc fires up the old girl and we burble back towards Wellington city, swing right and take a sweeping, scenic road around the curve of the harbour. There are motorboats, sleek, streamlined yachts, a tumble of white houses on the hills above, and sparkling, dancing seawater. It is all so achingly beautiful and real, all so far from Jeffrey and our apartment and my pain, that soon I am crying, and my terrible, awkward sobbing is impossible to stop. Huge, salty tears are splashing onto my shirt, over my hands and Linc's tan leather upholstery.

He swings the car into a layby, kills the engine, and pulls me into a hug. "Shh, shh," he says gently, but I can't help it.

I am howling into his cream linen shirt, dragging up great gulps of air, crying out my heart and my hatred and all the sorrow I have bottled up after the leaving, the loss, Jeffrey's constant betrayals, Mum's terrible death. All of it surging up now, inexplicably, perhaps none of it properly processed in my fear, my flight, my fancy for a new life.

"I'm sorry," I gasp, over and over, "I'm sorry," but Linc just clicks to me as though I'm a horse, and kisses the top of my head. I lean into his warmth, his strength, the indefinably familiar scent of him, and my paroxysms of sorrow slow. When I can breathe again, I realise suddenly how close he is. I sit up, blow my nose with a tissue, press my fingers to my hot cheeks.

"I'm so sorry, Lincoln. Really." And I realise it is the first time I've spoken his name aloud.

"Just call me Linc." His voice is husky. He clears his throat. I cannot read his expression as he releases me and leans back in his own seat. Is it reluctance? Awkwardness? Does he regret inviting me? "You looked so sad in the Roxy. I thought taking you for a drive round the coast would cheer you up. Maybe I was wrong."

"No, it was perfect." And I can tell that's got him confused. I feel like I want to cry again. I like this man, really like him – but he belongs to Sue, and we are supposed to be taking a casual drive into Wellington and just seeing the sights. Now I've gone and made things all strange. "I feel like I need to explain…"

"You don't need to explain anything."

"I do. You've been very kind." I can still feel the warmth of his fingers on my skin, his kiss on the top of my head. The idea that I was in this man's arms a minute ago is making me feel butterflies and terrified and sad, all at once. "I was in a terrible relationship… about as bad as you can imagine. I left him, but he put me through hell after that, and then my mum got sick. It's been a hard few years."

I feel like that's the understatement of the century, but no one wants the whole story. No one I've met yet, anyway.

"He must have really hurt you."

I can't answer that or I'll cry again. I shrug, and wrestle up a grin. "He's moved back to London, I've come to New Zealand, there's a lot of water between us now. I'll leave it at that, OK?"

"Alright." He shifts in his seat, looks out at the water, drums his long, brown fingers on the steering wheel. "How's your mum, now?"

There is a pause while I try to say, 'She passed away,' but then he sees my face and I don't need to tell him.

"Oh, jeeze, I'm sorry, Kate."

I figure Lori hasn't briefed him after all. I wonder if there is some kind of sadistic, obnoxious stormcloud following our old car today so that we can't find sunshine and lightness, even on this dazzlingly beautiful summer afternoon. *Yachts, harbour views, cute seaside bungalows, come on, seriously.*

I stuff my sodden tissues into my purse and draw a deep breath, haul my fingers through my hair and bundle it into a ponytail. I turn to look at him. Really look at him. I meet his eyes and see the caution in them, the tension in his body. He is not sure what to say, how to fix this, whether to take me straight home or go on with his plan for the day. He's not sure if I'm OK.

I don't know either, but I say brightly, "Wasn't there a plan to play music tonight?"

He rasps a hand through the stubble on his jaw. "There was, but we don't have to go."

"I want to." As Linc tilts his head and looks at me, undecided, I repeat, "I want to go."

The flash of his smile lifts that stormcloud and I bask in the hope that swirls in its wake. "I warn you, some of my muso mates are nuts. The music is sometimes brilliant, sometimes terrible. You don't know what you're getting into."

"How bad can it be?" I laugh. "Have you seen me on a good day?"

"Sometimes brilliant, sometimes terrible?" Linc grins.

"Exactly." And he is going with my riff on this one so I know we can still have fun, and I am smiling as he turns back to the wheel.

Linc starts the car, plants his foot, flicks the back out a little exuberantly as we come off the gravel and onto the tarmac. The engine snarls up through the gears then settles into a steady grumble as we roll through the city.

"Let's go play music. We'll find some food on the way."

We hunt and gather woodfired pizza from Jackson Street in Petone, and eat it sitting on a jetty in the late afternoon light. There are a few people fishing from the bollards along its length, the flash and whir of their lines and gentle murmur of their conversation a rhythmic backdrop to the sighing, restless sea.

Halfway along the jetty, there is a set of stairs and a platform and children are jumping into the water here, laughing, splashing, clambering out and running up the stairs to jump again.

Linc doesn't say much, except to point out some features in the harbour – the mouth of the Hutt River, Soames Island, the ferry to the South Island churning through the water as it rounds the peninsula and heads out across the Cook Strait. I am too far away to hear the pulse of its engines but I sense the freedom in its lines, the invitation that a ferry offers, *Come travel with me, we will cross the sea!*

This is peaceful, enjoyable, healing.

By the time we pull up near the blues bar on Main Street, the sun has slipped behind the range to the west and a cool breeze is skittering. The light fades late this time of the year. I drag on Olive's jacket as we step out of the car, and Linc pulls the bench seat forward to reveal a guitar case jammed behind. He swings it out, slams the door shut and locks it in one smooth motion, then reaches out to touch my shoulder. He looks into my face.

"Ready?" he asks. His hand is warm through my jacket. I nod, he grins, and then he's moving again, leading me up the street and opening a door for us to enter.

The street was quiet but the bar is jumping, full of people and noise. There are high ceilings, dim lights, rustic and eclectic furnishings. Heads turn as we emerge from the little lobby, and voices are raised above the din.

"Lincoln Brady, you devil, over here!"

"Good, the bass player's arrived."

Linc gestures with the guitar case. "I only brought the six-string."

"Never mind, you can play mine." A craggy fellow appears at our side, offering Linc a slender, burnished guitar with a long neck and four, gleaming strings.

Linc puts his own guitar down and reaches for it. "Thanks, Dave. Dave, this is Kate. Kate, this is Dave. And this is Hemi, George, Ira, over there is Mel, Dave's wife. Behind the bar is Jacqui, she owns this place."

I am smiling and shaking hands in a blur of faces, and soon Linc wanders off to plug his guitar in, in the half circle of space that serves as a stage.

Mel whisks me away to a table. "Come and sit with us, I'll get you a drink, what would you like, yeah, just put your purse down there with mine, this is Lollie, Mira and Rae, everyone knows everyone here and no one will bite, honest, so, it's nice to meet you."

Mel's chatter is a soothing balm. I put my jacket and handbag where she suggests, slide into a seat, take the drink she offers.

Lollie is a big-haired, big-laughing lady with lights strung all over her wheelchair and I warm to her at once. She tells me that her husband is away but tonight Rae pushed her all the way down Main Street to the bar, and Ira will give her a lift home later in his electrician's van. She shakes with mirth as she tells me how Rae couldn't lift Lollie over the kerb where the roadworks are, but Johnny Best helped them. Apparently, Johnny is quite a looker, so Lollie didn't mind him getting up close and personal. I get the feeling that everybody looks out for everybody in this quirky little place.

Mira is sleek and kohl-eyed, and watches me over the top of her glass with undisguised curiosity.

"So, how do you know Linc?" she asks. She is speaking to me, but her gaze slides past me to linger on Linc's tall, lean frame. I turn to look, too, and see he is tuning a couple of guitars with Hemi while Dave bustles about with leads and mike stands.

"Oh, he helps my sister with her farm."

Mira pouts. "I don't know why he does that kind of work. It's not like he needs to."

"Pardon?" But Mira just shrugs and I'm not sure I heard right, so I continue, "My sister lives near Mayton, I'm staying here for a while." I am anxious that these people don't think I am *really* with Linc, that I am moving in on Sue, and I am the kind of scarlet woman Jeffrey always said I was... I clamp down on my runaway thoughts, chastise myself for being dramatic. "Linc thought I might like to see more of Wellington. I've only been here a few weeks."

"Oh, how do you like it? Have you been on the Cable Car yet? You must go to the Te Papa museum soon." Mel has a million questions to keep me busy, but I can still sense Mira's mind on me while her gaze is on Linc.

Rae comes back to the table with packets of peanuts and crisps and dumps them in the middle. "Help yourself," she says magnanimously, then spins and yells at the stage, "Come on, you lot, where's the music? Lollie and I want to dance but at this rate we'll die of old age first!"

Linc laughs and Hemi shouts something unintelligible, then Dave steps up to a microphone. "Alright Rae, we'll get on with playing some numbers but only if you sing the first one."

"Yeah, sing *Wagon Wheel*," someone yells, and Rae throws up her arms.

"I'm not singing *Wagon Wheel*, Morrie, that's all you ever wanna hear. But I will do *Killing Me Softly*." And Rae steps into the circle of light and breathes the first few words into the microphone in a voice so like an angel I expect the strum of harps to follow.

Instead, Linc plays a bass run as light as a feather but deep as an ocean, and this mismatched little band goes on to deliver us the most heart-stoppingly beautiful rendition of that song that I have ever heard.

I am entranced. I feel reborn. After the emotional tumult of my afternoon, I feel Rae's voice wash over me like a balm, the music opening a door in my mind. Soothing, hopeful, exquisite. I watch Linc's long fingers caressing notes of love from his guitar, see him nod at Hemi as Rae finally steps back from the mike, hear them wrap this song like a gift and leave it, with the last tendrils of sound seeping away, at the doorstep of my heart.

I look at Linc, and know my eyes are shining with tears. Perhaps he understands how I feel about that song, those words tonight, because he holds my gaze. His eyes are deep and dark and I know I want to drown there. Ira bustles past to adjust the drumkit and the moment is broken, but I turn away feeling lighter than I have in years.

After that first song, Dave seems happy with the sound. He stops fiddling with leads and knobs and picks up a harmonica.

They play a nameless, instrumental blues number which warms everyone up, then Hemi starts in with the guitar opening for *Listen to the Music*. Linc comes in with the bass run, Ira on drums, and Hemi sings, "Don't you feel it growing, day by day."

Lollie yells, "Oh yeah!" from our table. Mel joins Hemi for the chorus, and they are soon laughing together with a Doobies-style exuberance which is catching.

Rae wheels Lollie out for a dance. "Come on, Kate, you too," she calls, and I find myself spinning on the dancefloor with Lollie, those swirling, twinkling lights on her wheels winking colour off the chrome on the bar stools, the instruments, the alabaster ceilings.

It is one of the most unexpectedly glorious nights of my life.

Not even Mira can spoil it when she asks Mel, during a lull in the music, why Linc didn't bring Sue tonight.

"Remember?" says Mel. "She's going global with that new product she told us about."

"Oh yes." Mira looks smug. "She asked for my advice on the colourways." And I realise how closely all these people are connected.

Our trip home in the dark is cold, but sparkling. My memory of the night's music has a champagne effect as I tuck my legs beneath me on the bench seat, snuggle into Olive's patchwork jacket and watch the starlit sky unfurl as we drive. I feel as though in the whole world tonight there is just this car, Linc, and me.

Pale light from the dashboard highlights Linc's profile and his soft cream shirt, just an arm's length away across the seat. Oddly for me, I want to touch him. I don't, and this doesn't dent my mood. It's past two in the morning when Linc drops me off at my Waiata gate, but I am still humming and smiling as I gather up my shoes and my purse and open the car door.

Linc touches my hand lightly, a spontaneous, friendly gesture. "I had fun tonight, thanks for coming along."

I flip my hand over, curl my fingers into his and feel a sexual charge flicker like lightning from my belly to the tips of my toes. From the startled burn in Linc's eyes, I know he's felt it, too.

Words catch in my throat as I stare at him, my cheeks on fire. "Um." I remember our tumultuous afternoon. "Thanks for... everything."

"All good," says Linc dismissively, but I am still holding his hand. My heart is racing, and the night has wrapped us in a cocoon of closeness. All we can do is stare at each other.

Abruptly, the spectre of Sue slides into view. I pull my fingers from his and slip out of the car. Linc watches me to the gate, I wave, and the Kingswood burbles away.

I tiptoe through dew-damp grass to my back door. "What a night," I tell my cold, dark house. *And what a man*. But I'm not telling anyone that.

Linc wants to sing as he leaves her house. But as he usually leaves singing to Rae and Hemi, he refrains. *She held my hand!* That beautiful, brave, sexy, intriguing woman!

Watching her lovely heart-shaped face tonight – so expressive when she forgot to guard it – and watching her dance had set something alight in his soul. After just a few songs she'd looked happy and her sparkling gaze had lit the room.

He was sorry that she'd cried, but he'd held her in his arms today for just a few moments and he wanted it to be forever.

Damn, but this could spell trouble. Wouldn't Sue be smug? He'd sworn to her he was happy.

Chapter 7

I spend the next day quietly, alone and absorbed in my manuscript. It is a drizzly day so I stay inside and play happy havoc with Lady Hatwick's marriage, writing a complex scene between Hattie and the elderly, emotionally distant Lord Hatwick. It involves his barely controlled outrage, her flippant indifference, and a breakfast of jam crumpets.

I am amazed at how armour-plated Hattie can be. Especially when the manly Duke Everland makes his manly appearance in the hall later, and she just brushes right past his throbbing manliness. She is warmed by strawberry jam and good, strong tea, and secure in her lust for her coachman. Heavens, if I don't watch it she'll be wanting to settle down soon and raise baby stablehands.

On Sunday, I wake to find it is raining hard and it is not just wet outside, but in. A large puddle has formed in my hallway and is expanding into the bedrooms.

"Oh, heavens!" I feel a rising panic, splash my way from Lavender into my office and ring the first person I think of.

"Linc here." His voice is gravelly from sleep.

I realise it's barely six, the dawn light just beginning to wash over the eastern hills, and I am momentarily paralysed. But I tell myself I'm not going to jump on him, I just need his help. "Sorry, I didn't realise it was so early."

"Kate?"

"Of course. I mean, yes! My house is flooding, do you think you could come and take a look?"

He is immediately practical. "Is it the roof, do you reckon, or the drains?"

"Um." I am looking, but I can't see anything obvious.

"Hang on, I'll come over."

While I await the burble of his ute, I attempt a cleanup with towels and a mop but soon give it up as a hopeless task. Water is appearing faster than my efforts can absorb it. I get my summer pyjamas soaked, so I change into a bra, oversized tee and sarong. I have just finished dressing when I hear the scrape of Linc's boots on the back porch and he walks in.

Linc lifts his chin in greeting then raises an eyebrow at my sarong. "Indonesia? Bali?"

"Bali. Girls' trip, years ago." *The girls all gone now, driven away by Jeffrey.* I think this is an odd greeting, but Linc heads down the hallway without further comment and surveys my growing freshwater lake.

"Fun," he grins. "Feel like a swim?"

Right now, I'd love to go swimming with Linc, go anywhere in fact, especially if it involves less clothing. But this may be impolitic to say, so I just trail after him as he searches for the cause of Waiata's inundation.

"Drains," he says at last, after a damp trudge through all the rooms, then around the outside of the house. "Got a shovel?"

"Sorry?" I am distracted, studying his profile as he studies the ground and the crumbling, plastered foundations. He mistakes my vagueness for worry.

"Never mind." He heads back to his ute, drags out two shovels and hands one to me. "This can be fixed, Kate, you won't drown in your bed tonight. The drains have been blocked by pine roots, that's all. We'll have to dig 'em out." He pauses a moment and looks at my bare feet. "You might want to put some boots on."

So, I spend my morning in gumboots and a sarong, digging out drains alongside Linc. Our progress is slow and we are soon soaked by the rain and covered in mud. It seems as fast as we dig, the holes fill up and the waterlogged sides collapse. However, after two hours of hard yakka, as they say, we reopen the old drains designed to divert rainflow away from the homestead and solve my flooding problem.

I enjoy working with Linc. He is easy company. He doesn't talk much but he's observant, and notices when I am struggling. A couple of times he leans over without comment to help me move a heavy rock, or slice through a tree root blockage.

I look for any uneasiness in Linc after Friday, but he seems his usual self. He doesn't appear worried that I might burst into tears without warning, or tell him my whole life story. And we touch only once, accidentally, when we swap shovels. He just glances at me, then keeps on working. My fingers are tingling and I know my cheeks are bright red.

Blimey, Kate, get over yourself. But I can't, because it'd mean getting over him.

I find I am fascinated by Linc. I catch myself watching his hands, his expressions, the way he lifts the shovel, walks, moves, and jumps from the tray of his ute after he's put the tools away. I store these images in my mind so I can write them down later. My coachman is modelled on Linc, and I find the two are becoming dangerously blurred. I have to make a mental note that it is Lady Hatwick, not me, who is sleeping with Linc – although he is a decade older and lives 200 years in the past – so I mustn't get carried away.

Regardless, after we've saved the house I invite him in for breakfast. Or lunch, or something. I have a brief flashback to weekend brunches with Jeffrey at our local, inner-city café, with him flirting with the wait staff and swanning about, showing off his latest acquisition – the latest customised iPhone, an expensive watch, a new car... And no one cared, to be honest. They either had it all, too, or were so hard up they never imagined they could, but Jeffrey didn't understand that.

I reflect that there is a lot Jeffrey doesn't understand.

Linc is speaking. "Do you have a towel I can use to clean up a bit?" I blink back to the present to realise he is still standing, drenched and muddy, on my doorstep.

I feel unaccountably reckless. "Even better, I have a shower. Want to borrow it?"

Linc flashes me his warm, sudden smile. "Sounds good."

He strips off his oilskin vest and boots and follows me into the house. I find him fluffy towels and new soap and point him in the direction of the bathroom. He closes the door but doesn't latch it and I hear the shower running, imagine the steam on the mirror, hot water running down his lean, tanned body... I rest my forehead weakly against the wall.

Heaven help me.

Then I realise he'll be out soon, so I skip off to the kitchen to put the kettle on and gather salad items out of the fridge. I strip free of my muddy clothes in the Rose room's tiny ensuite, and towel myself down. I am feeling far more civilised, passing Linc's bathroom door in new blue jeans and a boho peasant blouse, when he emerges.

Linc bumps into me, apologises, and catches my hand in his. *On purpose?* I am not sure. My heart stops when I look into his face. His hair is damp and adorably spiky, his eyes that deep, soulful, dark brown that devours me.

"Tomato bruschetta and a Greek salad?" I ask brightly, and he blinks.

"Primo," he says, and I make my escape to the kitchen.

Once there, I tell myself in no uncertain terms to stop being a fool for this man, while slathering garlic butter onto the bruschetta like there is no tomorrow. I set Linc to tearing up the leaves of a cos lettuce, we scatter olives, feta cheese and tiny tomatoes throughout, then carry it all into the lounge room. No outdoor dining today, it is too wet and cool. I place everything on the mahogany coffee table in the centre of the room, with a view through the bay windows.

Linc takes the couch and I settle for the worn, leather club chair nearby. We are just looking at each other and I am wondering how to start a conversation without leaping into his lap and kissing him – where on earth did that thought come from? – when there is the splashy rush of tyres, a toot-toot, and Olive arrives.

I have never been so disappointed and yet so glad to see her.

"Hello!" she calls in a sing-song voice, as I let her in through the French doors. "Ooh, Linc, you're here too, how lovely!" Olive turns to me. "I came to check you weren't being flooded. Last time we had rain like this, Waiata Homestead became a lake. It took Lori and I a week to clean it up."

"Well, that's why Linc's here," I explain. "I woke up to the beginnings of a lake, but he helped me clear the drains and we've diverted all the water."

"Excellent, excellent, no worries then." She looks at the spread of food on the table, Linc looking relaxed on the couch, perhaps also his wet hair and my flustered, nervous manner. "Well, I'll be on my way now."

"No, Olive, please stay, there's enough for all of us. Take a seat, I'll make more coffee."

Olive can never resist food, so she is soon settled on the couch next to Linc, and by the time I return they are having an uproarious conversation about Olive's last trip to Africa. I find the meal passes pleasantly, with the three of us comparing travel stories and laughing at Olive's outrageous, seemingly frequent brushes with mayhem and death.

Linc looks comfortable in her company and obviously knows her well. Occasionally, he prompts Olive to tell a story he's already heard, with a, "Go on, Kate will love that one." Once, he rests a hand on her shoulder and says, "Olive, for the sake of international relations and the future of our planet, please do not go hitchhiking in eastern Europe again."

Olive is tickled by his request and waves her hands about airily. "Oh, Lincoln darling, that was another era. I won't go again." Her eyes twinkle. "But I'd love to go to South America.

And to see polar bears in Alaska. You know, before they disappear, the poor things."

That prompts Linc to talk about his months in Alaska during an OE to North America, and I enjoy letting his voice wash over me, my eyes straying to watch his face, his hands, my mind following the word pictures that he and Olive trace. Eventually, and perhaps inevitably, the conversation turns to horses.

"I've been working with that big grey of Fletcher's. He's going so well, just primo. He's quiet, responsive, nothing bothers him, he's almost as good as Dash to work with."

"And Dash is a lot older, more experienced," Olive observes. "That's impressive."

"Yeah, I'm thinking of keeping him. Fletcher wants the bay mare back but not the gelding."

"I'd like to learn more about training horses," I say, surprising myself. *Kate, you are feeling bold today*. But I am also thinking of my coachman and the things I need to know to do him justice.

"And I'd like to meet this horse," exclaims Olive. "Kate, how about we go together to watch one day, when Linc brings him into the pen? Linc, will that work for you?"

Linc turns his warm gaze on me. "Yeah, that'll work." I feel the irresistible flit of butterflies in my belly, and give him a fleeting smile.

We arrange to visit his round pen after the bookshop closes on Thursday next. Olive soon flits off through the curtain of rain to her little car, and her tail-lights disappear into the deluge. We are alone again.

I leap up, take our plates to the kitchen and pop them in the sink. I turn to find myself eyes to chest with Linc, who's followed me in with the coffee mugs.

"Oops," I say, stepping sideways. But then I catch the look in his eyes and I am lost.

"Kate." His voice is husky. He smells amazing this close. To my absolute surprise, I lift my face to his and... kiss him.

I think Linc is surprised too, but he kisses me back. He is restrained at first, but when I open my eyes and smile, he cups my face with his hands and leans in. He kisses me teasingly, tasting my lips, tracing my tongue with his. My heart is hammering, my senses overwhelmed, and I dissolve in the depths of his sweet, sweet embrace as he deepens the kiss. He tastes irresistible. He feels divine.

I feel like I've been starving for years, and I want to live in this moment for ever.

Linc makes a small, guttural sound and gathers me close, his touch tracing fire beneath my cotton shirt. I am on tippy toes now, moulding my curves to his, my fingers tangled in his hair, my body pressed against him. I want him wrapped around me, I want to absorb him, love and indulge him with every fibre of my being. I am completely absorbed, kissing him in the middle of my farmhouse kitchen, when a tiny, red warning light flashes in the back of my mind...

Sue.

Bloody hell. I jump as if I've been stung, pull back and bump my head on the wall.

"Jeeze, Kate," Linc's voice is hoarse, his gaze still dark with desire. "Are you alright?"

"I'm sorry, I shouldn't have done that."

"What?" He clears his throat and steps back. "Which bit, exactly?"

"I think you'd better go. I'm sorry." *Oh, Kate, you idiot.* I am feeling ashamed and stupid now, trying not to cry, cursing my impulsiveness.

He looks puzzled. "Alright, but I'd rather stay to…"

"Ohhh, no," I breathe, staring at the floor. "No, you have to go."

"…find out what I… Oh, hell." Linc rubs his hand frustratedly through his hair and turns to leave. He waits a long, silent second until I look up at him. His look is troubled. "I'm sorry, Kate, if I made you uncomfortable."

Oh, Linc. "Thankyou for helping me today." My voice sounds very small.

"Sweet as," he says, but his tone is polite now. He nods awkwardly. "See you round." I listen to the scuff of his boots in the porch, the startup rumble of his car, then I slide down the wall right where I am and curl up on the damp floorboards.

I feel battered by my roller coaster of emotions. I wonder what I have ruined.

Linc drives as far as the front gate of the farm and pulls up, the ute's engine pulsing gutturally at idle. He runs his hands down his face in a gesture of despair, then thunks his forehead defeatedly against the steering wheel. *Damn, I fucked that up. I don't know what the hell I did, but I fucked it up.*

He recalls her body against his, her sweet curves and her willing mouth, and groans in frustration. After a long minute he opens his eyes, takes a deep breath and shifts into first, moving out onto the highway.

I cry a lake of tears and almost drown my house again. Then I decide I can't stand the idea of being alone tonight. I get up, take a long, hot shower with the shadow of Linc alongside, and ring Lori.

"If I bring dinner, can I come over? Say, about six?"

"You're welcome anytime, Kate, you know that." Lori sounds tired but pleased to hear from me. "Do you want me to pick you up in the car? It's raining buckets out there."

"No, I'll manage, thanks. It'll be vegetarian lasagna for mains, but I'll make a dessert to sweeten the deal." I know Lori's boys are enthusiastic carnivores and won't be overly excited about the lasagna.

Lori laughs and we hang up.

I browse through my mother's old recipe books and find one for a lemon syrup dessert cake. I know I have plenty of lemons from the orchard, and vanilla icecream to serve with it. I spend the afternoon baking my cake, layering the lasagna, dreaming about Lady Hatwick and her coachman and trying grimly not to think about Linc. Fortunately, I have lots of work to do on their relationship arc because, thanks to Lori and our conversation a week or two ago, my original plot sketch for this novel did not include a coachman.

Taika meets me at their door wearing an enormous yellow hard hat, and towing Nikau on a blanket. Nikau is dressed in a Spiderman suit and holding one leg dramatically in the air.

"I am Spideyman Search and Wescue, and Nikki bwoke his yeg," Taika intones.

"Oh dear," I say, dripping on the doorstep with my picnic basket. "I'm so glad you rescued Spiderman, what would we do without him? Can I help you bandage him up?"

Nikau is tickled by this idea and waves his leg at me, hopefully.

"No, Penny is magic, she will yick him all better," Taika assures me, and he tows his brother off to be ministered to by the magic collie dog in the backyard.

I head into the kitchen, shedding my gumboots and rain jacket as I go. Lori is tossing a salad while Tommo stands beside her on a box, throwing wedges of gouda into the mix. I pop my cake on the bench, icecream into the freezer and lasagna into the oven, then give Tommo a big hug. I look at my sister over the top of his curly, dark head.

"All good?" I ask, and she grins to hear this much-used Kiwi term coming from me, a Pom who turned Aussie for years.

"All good," she says, and joins our hug. Tommo wriggles out from between us and runs to join the boys outside. Lori steps back and looks at me.

"You look tired tonight, Katie," she says. "Worried, maybe."

"I tidied my eyebrows and put lip gloss on," I laugh. "Are you telling me it didn't do a thing?"

Lori shakes her head. "It just seems like you've been carrying the weight of the world since you arrived. Happy sometimes, of course, but always with a sort of... shadow."

"A shadow? Nice." I wonder what happened to that lovely bubble of lightness I felt at the Blues Club on Friday night and into the weekend. Then I remember. *Oh, yeah. And you've no one to blame but yourself, Kate, because you kissed him first.*

Lori flicks her ponytail at me as she swishes off to check the oven. "I wondered if it was because of your mum... or Jeffrey. Or maybe both. But I didn't want to say anything in case it made you sad."

Lori has her back to me so I have time to hide the tears that leap to my eyes, before she turns around. *Dear Mum.* But to be honest, I do feel lighter. Even with these tears. Even with my confusion over Linc. I don't feel anymore like I'm fighting back a grief so huge it will swallow me. My tears tonight are nothing like those I spilled in Linc's car. They just feel like an acknowledgement that I miss Mum, and will always miss her.

"To be honest, Lori, I cried so much a few days ago that I don't think I have many more tears left. And don't worry, I'll be OK." I shrug, as Lori's huge eyes fix on me.

"Oh, Kate, I'm sorry I wasn't there for you!"

"Um, I was fine..." I shift uncomfortably, hoping she doesn't ask me for details, hoping that Linc hasn't talked to anyone because then my sister will have questions for sure.

Fortunately, the three boys choose that moment to come hurtling into the kitchen. Tommo is in pursuit of Taika who is in pursuit of Nikau, who has stolen the rescue towel.

"Give it back, I have to wescue you!"

"I don't wanna be wescued. Mum, he's twying to wescue me!"

"Taika took my hat, he says it's a magic hat. Mum, tell Taika to wear his own hat! And Nikau let the dog lick his face, it was so gross..."

"Boys, boys..." It takes us a couple of minutes to wrangle the unruly trio into the bathroom to wash their hands for dinner, at which point Gus walks in the front door and they run to repeat their grievances to him.

Lori looks at Gus and rolls her eyes. He scoops up the twins and I grab Tommo's hand, and we march everyone to the dining table to eat. My lasagna is deemed delicious by my sister and Gus and passable by the boys after they've slathered it in tomato sauce. We talk about their upcoming trip to visit Gus's parents, and what superhero we would most like to be, and of course Lori asks if the homestead flooded at all, after this amazing rain.

"Yes, it flooded, but Lincoln helped me dig out the drains this morning and everything is great now," I enthuse. At my mention of Linc, a look passes between Lori and Gus, and I wonder if I should have toned it down a bit. To distract everyone, I offer dessert.

My lemon syrup cake with ice cream is a massive hit. Afterwards, I volunteer to be on bath and bedtime story duty, so Gus and Lori head for the lounge with a glass of wine each.

I'm glad they have some time to relax together, but I get the feeling all they did was talk about me, because they stop immediately when I come into the room. Gus jumps up to go and cuddle his boys goodnight, and Lori fixes me with a look.

"Why didn't you tell me Linc Brady was helping you dig the drains? Gus could have brought the little digger down and saved you all that shovelwork."

"It all just... happened," I say, shrugging. *Actually, quite a bit happened.*

"It's fine, it's just that... Well, I feel I need to warn you about Lincoln." Lori looks uncomfortable.

"Warn me?" I wonder if she's about to tell me he has three heads, it's just that two of them are invisible, or he turns into a werewolf on a full moon.

"Yes. Lincoln is very... popular around here. He is attractive, clever, capable, independently wealthy..."

"He is?" He doesn't look wealthy. A memory niggles at me and I wonder if Olive has mentioned something.

"...and people like to watch him. They... talk. Everyone watches everyone around here, they all talk about each other too, but you'll find Linc is in the middle of more than his fair share of rumours."

I frown because I'm not quite sure where she's going with this. Lori takes this for disapproval. "I'm sorry, I don't want to upset you, but I heard from Olive that you went into Wellington with Linc last week. You're new here and just starting to make friends, and I don't want you to get hurt."

"What?" I am instantly defensive. After my afternoon of self-flagellation, I really don't need my sister piling onto the cart as well. "He just showed me round the city then we went to a blues bar, that's all!" *And I cried on his shoulder and he held my hand then today I kissed him, but I'm not telling you any of that.*

"I don't know why he's always at the centre of the stories, Kate, it may just be other people's jealousy, but I'm worried that where there's smoke, there's fire. You've had so much heartache already. And you need to know that he is living with..."

I jump in. "I know, I know, Lori, I'm fully aware that it's complicated. I just went out for the day with him because Olive

said it'd be a good idea and he was nice enough to ask me."
I am speaking all in a rush and I can feel my cheeks burning,
my heart pounding, my mind unusually clear and angry.
"Seriously, you'd think I'd just gone and gotten engaged to the
bloke."

Lori looks at me, astonished, and then laughs. "You're
right, this is ridiculous. Maybe we all just get a bit
over-sensitive, living in this small town." She jumps up, wraps
me in a huge hug, then drags me down to the couch. "Sit. Now,
tell me how you're going with Lady Hatwick's love life."

Relieved that she is no longer asking about mine, I keep
Lori entertained with stories of Hattie's hay-festooned,
romantic interludes until Gus comes in. He looks exhausted, as
he often does, so I excuse myself and wander home down the
long, dark driveway.

Chapter 8

Monday is quiet. Lori has taken the kids to Wellington to see her in-laws and I have far too much time alone to think. I should be writing, but instead I ramble about in my still-damp house and garden and not much gets done until mid-afternoon, when I have a mad frenzy of creativity and write two steamy sex scenes. They are unlinked to the main story as yet, but I have hope for them. Lady Hatwick is in an absolute lather over her coachman, but completely unable to confide in anyone because of the forbidden nature of their relationship. I am able to empathise.

Evening finds me curled up on my wrought iron bench in a sweatshirt and my sarong. I am nursing a glass of wine and a heart full of shame and have convinced myself that I am a loose woman with no morals. Worse than that, I am a totally damaged one, because all I could do when a nice man took me for a scenic drive around the coast was burst into tears and smudge my mascara all over his shirt.

I tell myself that Linc did not deserve to have my sob story foisted on him. And he didn't ask to be leapt upon yesterday, in my kitchen, then unceremoniously kicked out of the house. I tell myself that holding someone's hand or kissing him when he belongs to another may not be wickedness to the level of, say, Lady Hatwick's, but it could well be a slippery slope and a path to ruin. I tell myself that I should focus on my writing instead, that all other activities are frivolous and will not help me achieve my life goals.

At this point I am wrong on almost every count and should just go to bed. Instead, I drink the rest of the bottle, reel into my study, go online and google my ex.

I am still smarting over what I have learned when Olive picks me up in the morning.

"Good morning!" she sings, wrenching her car into first and hurtling off down my driveway like a little green bat out of hell. "How are you today? I am going vegan, I've decided, but I'm not sure my cat wants to be vegan so I'll have to research that a bit more. He was very unimpressed with his dinner last night."

I let Olive's chatter wash over me while I think about Jeffrey. His company is in trouble, the Times said, and there is talk of fraud and embezzlement. No surprises there, but if he can't sort it out my name may get dragged through the mud, too.

Jeffrey has never signed divorce papers, even after three years apart and a world of bitterness. My Sydney lawyer is still chasing him. Yet another act of control, I reflect with anger, keeping me legally tied to him while I fight desperately to be free, and he flaunts his wealth and freedom. My online research had showed him tripping about London with every pretty, young socialite naive enough to think he's a good catch.

Some of the old fear is creeping back, I can feel it. And I detest him for it.

As we hurtle into Mayton along Main Street, Olive says something about checking her post box. She sweeps into a parking space, drags up the hand brake with a screech, leaps out and trips off into a nearby lane. I sit still, in the sudden quiet.

Through the front windscreen, I can see the Carlisle sisters unlocking their shops and getting organised for the day. It is early, but Linc's ute is also parked a little further along the street. He is loading chaff bags into it from the stockfeed store nearby.

I feel like ducking down so he can't see me, I am still so upset about the other day – but then I spot Billie Carlisle approaching Linc. I pause to watch, intrigued. The way her hand reaches out to grip his jacket, the way she tilts her head and sparkles as she steps in to him, it is clear she is besotted. *Really?* I hadn't known. *Does everybody fall for this guy?*

To my surprise, Billie reaches up and kisses Linc on the mouth. Not just a peck either, but a solid, inviting, 'Take me if you want me' kiss. I freeze. I wait for Linc to brush her off, but instead he leans in close to speak with her. She pouts, he grins, then she pirouettes back to her antiques shop and he returns to stacking his truck.

I sit in Olive's car, blushing now with shame and mortification. *Has he arranged to meet her later?* Lori was right. There is fire here, for sure. I just wish I wasn't left spluttering in the smoke.

Olive comes back. She picks up her story where she left off, chattering away as we tear round the corner to park behind the bookshop. I start up the coffee machine and we get on with our day, but I feel like I am on automatic, anxious and disillusioned. I don't see Linc, I don't see Billie either, and that's probably a good thing – all the hells I'd imagined for pert, pretty Christa in a bad moment look tame now compared to the things I'd do to Billie if I saw her.

I chide myself for being uncharitable. What claim do I have over Linc? I've only just turned up here. Billie's lived here for years, they might go way back. And maybe Sue knows, who knows? Relationships these days, and all that.

Although Linc had struck me as a steady, one woman type… Just goes to show what *I* know.

Cheered by this depressing thought, I drag myself through the afternoon. Daisy the Cat Lady turns up with three kittens tucked into her bosom, and I pat their soft-furred heads while handing over her mochaccino with extra sugar. Old Vaughan arrives for his usual 3pm latte, catches me doing this and makes some dreadful remark about wanting to stroke the kittens, too.

Brad is in earshot and chokes on his coffee, while I exclaim, "Manners, mister!"

Daisy laughs at my outrage, links her arm with Vaughan's and drags him off down the street. He beams at her, and she chatters away, sharing her mochaccino, and occasionally patting or tucking in her bosomful of cats. At last sight, the ginger kitten had escaped entirely and was climbing into her hair.

It's a funny old world. I help Olive clean up and lock up, then we hurtle home in her little car to my sprawling, old house.

"Do you think my cat would like to go vegan?" Olive asks. "He's a very New Age cat, it might suit him. Is there vegan fish?"

Good heavens. I put on a stern face. "Cats need meat and fish. Your cat must not go vegan, Olive, he will die."

"Oh, that'd be a shame. Never mind, *I'm* finding it very beneficial, did I tell you that my rash has gone? Look, you can see how the..." Olive starts pulling up her shirt.

I'm not sure I want to know. "Were you thinking to make your huskies vegan, too?"

"Oh no," Olive laughs, her rash forgotten. "If I tried that, they'd probably break into my house and eat the cat!"

I laugh and wave goodbye, then head straight inside. On top of that Times' article bombshell last night, today has been too much. Irrationally, I feel like Linc has rejected me and it is a slap in the face, all because I saw Billie kiss him. I sigh, and reach for icecream, my ugg boots and my laptop. I want to eat, write and sleep.

I keep my head down and do this all the rest of the week. It is a solitary existence, but I just don't want to see anyone for a while. On the weekend, I visit Lori to update her on my latest juicy chapters. Lady Hatwick has told the manly Duke Everland to go to hell, and is on the verge of telling her husband much the same thing.

I walk home on Sunday night with a warm glow. I am OK. I don't need Linc. I haven't thought about Mum for an entire day. I will ring my lawyer in the morning and razz her about Jeffrey.

I am strong, I am healing. I will get through this.

I have some success with my lawyer when I phone her on Monday morning. She vows to chase up what's going on in London and tell me if there's anything I can do to avoid being hauled into Jeffrey's mess. When I left him, I gave up everything just to get the hell out of there, but we are still legally tied and I'm afraid that might ensnare me somehow.

To keep from dwelling on what could happen, I get busy with what I can do right now. I go shopping. It is Lori's birthday next week, and I want to check out the craft shop and gallery in the old library building in town.

I borrow Lori's car, drive into Mayton and park by the beautifully restored, century-old pub in the main street. I walk up the street in a sunflower-print sundress and heels, feeling ridiculously urbanised and free after my long days of self-isolation on the farm. This is hilarious to me, someone who has lived in central London, and I can't help smiling as I step into the cool, sturdy, quiet building in a garden setting.

A woman is walking out through the foyer as I approach, a statuesque, blue-eyed blonde in a floral dress, with metal callipers on her legs and a companion dog at her side. I step aside to allow them both unimpeded access to the steps. She smiles as she walks by, and I glance casually after her. Linc's ute is pulling into a parking space out front.

I see the blonde woman wave to him. Linc nods and walks around his vehicle to open the passenger door for her. He is focussed on the woman and does not notice me at first. The woman, who must surely be Sue, says something animated and he grins. His reply makes her laugh. Then his gaze flicks past her shoulder and he sees me.

Linc raises his hand in greeting. I feel like a deer caught in the headlights. He starts forward as if to approach me and I duck into the gallery, striding quickly through the first room and then the next. I cannot face meeting Linc with Sue there. And I'm not sure I can face meeting Sue at all. I am here to shop, to browse through art and craft exhibits, to find a gift for my sister, to try to be normal and not complicated for once. *Is that too much to ask?*

Linc does not follow me, and soon I hear the distant burble of the Kingswood pulling out. My heart is beating fast and I feel unbearably anxious. It is ages before I can drag my focus back to the present and do justice to the display before me.

It is a well-appointed gallery, full of objects crafted with skill and artistry. I select a fine, carved timber bowl which Lori can use for entertaining, and a colourful woollen rug for her floor. I know Taika and Nikau decorated the last one with black house paint they'd scavenged from Gus's shed. I walk up to the counter and one of the elder Carlisle sisters emerges from a back room. Derryn, I think.

I find myself having to smile and be sociable. *Small-town life is complex*, I decide upon leaving, and head straight to the pub for a drink.

It is not yet lunchtime, but I don't care. I sit outside on the sunlit terrace with a glass of house wine, foccacia bread, and antipasto. At another outdoor table, I can see Dick Trelaney with a suntanned woman I presume to be his wife, Nessa, and his cute, mini-me son. The couple are laughing together while their son plays under the table with a lean, panting sheepdog.

Seeing Trelaney gets me thinking about my garden, and the old homestead I am viewing more as a haven each day. I decide that I should get organised to renovate it a little. This will give me a practical project and perhaps get me out of my own head. A writer's life can be lonely and introspective, I've realised, and may not be good for me longterm. Last week was so quiet, I feel I've become a hermit.

After a moment, I reflect that struggling with the ethical challenge of being wildly attracted to someone else's man is not helping me either. I have Lincoln at a long arm's length at present, but it feels like a hiatus rather than an ending. Perhaps Lady Hatwick has been a bad influence?

The food was delicious, the wine has completely relaxed me, and I wander inside to pay the bill. After the glare of the sun, it is cool and dark inside the hotel and the woman at the till smiles at me. "Did you enjoy your lunch?"

"Yes, thankyou."

"It's perfect weather for sitting outside today."

I nod, and pay the bill, and I'm sliding my card back into my purse when I hear the unmistakable sound of Linc's chuckle across the room. My eyes leap to look of their own accord.

Over the woman's shoulder, I see Linc pulling out a chair. A dark-haired woman slides into it – I know her, that's Mira from the Blues Club! As she sits, she catches his hand and presses it to her lips. He pauses on his way to his own seat, leans down and lightly kisses her cheek. The gesture is familiar, and Mira is glowing, and I am so shocked I forget to take the lunch receipt the woman offers me.

"Your receipt, ma'am?"

I mutter something unintelligible, take the flimsy thing and plunge blindly for the door.

I curse myself all the way down the street to where I parked Lori's car. By the time I reach the big, old gumtree by the church, I calm down a little and begin to see the incident as a positive. As I slide into the driver's seat and turn over the engine, I think desperately, *Sue and Mira in the same day!* Surely this will cure me of any untoward feelings for Linc.

I feel sad, annoyed, and reckless enough to go to the hardware store on my way home. I don't know anything about hardware stuff, but I need a distraction. *Am I using retail therapy to feel better? Yes, but too bad.* I am a bit hazy about my renovating goals, but old Vaughan works there and he's a mine of information.

Vaughan wheezes his way around the aisles ahead of me, piling my cart high. I buy sandpaper for the flaking windowsills, various pots of paint, drop cloths, rollers, and draught strips. I am hazy on how to use everything, but I tumble into the car with it all and drive back to Lori's, imagining that either Gus or Google can educate me.

It turns out to be Google because Gus is delayed in Christchurch for an extra night, solving a supplier problem. I search up how to refurbish old timber windowsills and doors. Then, because the back porch seems the most often-used of all the entrances to my farmhouse, I start with that.

"You will get your turn," I promise the Waiata gate.

By the time I've run out of daylight, I have sanded back the faded blue door and two flaking windowsills. I feel physically tired and gritty all over, but oddly content. I leave my tools beside the woodpile ready for tomorrow, and head for the shower.

I still have nagging concerns about Jeffrey's financial dramas in London. I have a grim sense of loss after seeing Linc with Sue today, and lingering shock at his liaison with Mira – in broad daylight! Meanwhile, Lady Hatwick is still waiting for me to finalise her most recent altercation with her husband.

Yet I roll into bed thinking, *Despite everything, today has been a constructive day*.

Chapter 9

The following afternoon, Olive reminds me we'd planned to go and see Linc's grey horse, after work. I try but I can't think of a good excuse to wriggle out. She must notice how noncommittal I sound now, after I'd been so keen a week or two ago, but she is determined we will go.

We lock up the bookshop, hop into Olive's car and roar out along a gravel road to a big gateway with sturdy totara posts, on the far outskirts of town. There is a prancing horse carved into the gate.

"What a clever carving!" I exclaim.

Olive steers to the right and hurtles through, barely missing the left post. "Linc's mother made it. She was amazing with timber, and she really loved horses. Linc keeps it oiled so it stays looking good."

I think of my battered, old timber gate at Waiata and renew my vow to give it some love and care. Then I notice a mossy timber sign nestled among the shrubs, announcing in bronze letters that this is 'Summer Homestead.'

"Ohhh, the Brady's Summer Homestead." I feel like a fool. *How could I not have remembered Linc's surname?*

"Yes," smiles Olive, putting her foot down along the tree-lined driveway. "This is a big farm, owned for generations, and Summer Homestead is named for the time of year its gardens look best. Rae's wedding will be held here this weekend."

"Rae's wedding?" I didn't think Lori had mentioned a name.

"Rae and Hemi. They've been friends with Linc and Sue since forever. The Summer Homestead is a very exclusive venue, and the gardens are amazing."

"So I've been told," I mutter, but Olive is off, gushing about the roses, as we sweep up the long, curving drive and into view of the house.

All I can do is stare. Olive was right, it *is* gorgeous. *Linc lives here?* I remember Lori's comment about him being independently wealthy. *Blimey. She wasn't kidding.*

We skid to a stop in front of a huge, impeccably restored, three-storey villa. The immaculate weatherboards are pale blue, fronted by an extensive white porch beneath a dove-grey roof. There are luxuriant roses growing against the verandah steps and bordering the expansive, sandstone terraces each side of the house. The garden beds are magnificent, all the standard bushes and climbers bearing huge, double, pink and mauve blooms.

To the right, falling gently away towards the river, an extensive garden with elegant specimen trees offers a sophisticated blend of light, shade, and colour. I wonder if Dick Trelaney looks after this garden, too. Or perhaps Sue is a gardener? It is all beautifully maintained.

I turn to ask Olive, but she is already out of the car and disappearing round the left side of the house. Beyond the villa is a neat collection of stables and yards, and Olive heads there at an enthusiastic trot. I trail after her, feeling awkward to be here, like some kind of interloper. I wonder if Sue is home.

Then I spot Linc in the yards. As always, despite my best effort I am captivated by the sight of him. Tall and lean, he is wearing dusty jeans and a black tee, with a rope looped over his shoulder. Crinkling his eyes against the glare, he is entirely focused on the horse in the yard with him.

The grey horse is cantering around the inside edge of the yard, his powerful body moving steadily forward, his eye and ear on Linc in the centre. Every time the horse slows a little, Linc raises his arm in a smooth motion and clicks with his tongue, and the animal goes back to his steady pace. There is no rope between Linc and the horse, just body language and Linc's soft clicking, and each is focused intently on the other.

After a few minutes, Linc steps back and brings his arm down. The horse slows, turns in towards him, and stops – then shies violently at Olive's hat.

Linc looks round. "Hello, Olive. You look like a fruit salad."

"Lincoln, dear, you're always full of compliments."

"Kate." Linc nods in acknowledgement as I appear. He studies me and smiles, but it is polite, distant, not the smile he shared with Sue, or Mira. Or his smile in my kitchen when we kissed.

I don't know if I am pleased or saddened by that. Half of me is grateful for his help the other day with my flooded house, the other half is annoyed that I needed it. I climb a rail next to Olive, and settle to watch Linc working the horse. Olive is excited about the whole thing and gives me a running commentary.

"He is asking the horse to move away from him, that's when it canters around the circle, see? When he steps back and lowers his arm, the horse knows he can come in. Look, the horse comes into the centre, lowers his head and licks and chews, see that movement? That's the horse telling Lincoln he is listening, he wants to be with him, he accepts him as a leader, but through trust and respect, not fear."

I watch Linc rubbing the horse's face and ears with his strong fingers, speaking with him softly. Then he unloops the rope from his shoulder and slides it over the horse's nose. With deft hands, Linc fashions a rope halter, with a rein looping from one side of the horse's muzzle to the other.

"Now, he is working on left and right," Olive explains. "See, he pulls the left rein very gently, just until the horse responds and tucks his head to the left. Then he lets the horse move his head back, relax, then he asks again. He will do this again and again. Repetition is key. Later, perhaps even on another day, he will work on the right rein."

It seems to me that this is long, slow work requiring incredible patience. "Why does he ask the same thing over and over? It must take ages."

"Because if you teach it enough times, it becomes an automatic response. If Lincoln is riding that horse one day, galloping along, and he has to turn fast, he needs the horse to respond without argument or confusion, just do it."

"Do you train your huskies like that?"

That prompts a huge smile from Olive. "Oh yes, and I love training my huskies! I learn so much from them along the way. Don't you think, Lincoln? We learn so much?"

"Yep," is Linc's brief answer. "And I find every horse is different." At that, he takes a sideways glance at me. I recall our tumultuous meetings full of tears, music, kisses and rejection, and I flush scarlet.

"Linc," I ask abruptly, wondering if he's just compared me to a horse, "could you train this horse to harness?"

He looks up, interested. "In time, yes. Why?"

"Well, in my novel, Lady Hatwick has this thing with a coachman, so I'd like to know more about how he'd drive horses in harness. You know, how it works, what it's like."

Linc thinks about that for a moment while he does his gentle, repetitive training, asking for a left turn, getting it, releasing the rein, then asking again. "A coachman, huh?"

"Yes." I tilt my chin, daring him to laugh.

"What era are we talking?"

"Late 1700's, early 1800's."

"This 'Lady Hatwick' is allowed to have a thing with a coachman, then?" There is a trace of the old, familiar sparkle in Linc's eyes. I feel suddenly like I've always felt with Linc – easy, comfortable, his warm humour bubbling up to embrace us like a hug.

I roll my eyes. "Absolutely not. But she does anyway. Can you show me a horse working in harness?"

"Well, this boy is a way off doing anything as sophisticated as that, but Dash could. I've had her dragging bailage around the paddock so it won't be hard to teach her more."

Olive coos over the idea, getting excited about the possibilities of us all trotting through Mayton in a carriage with a matching pair. Linc gives the grey a rest, then leads him through the yard gate.

He offers the leadrope to me. "Want to take him to the paddock?"

"What? No. I won't know how to do it right." I still have Jeffrey's voice in my head. *You can't do it. You're so useless.*

Linc's tone is reassuring. "You just lead him. Gently on a loose rein, like this." I must still look dubious because he adds, "Come on, I'll walk with you."

"Don't mind me," Olive grins, "I'll just go and bring the car round."

I frown at her, but I take the rope, and immediately I feel a silent communion with the horse. I step forward and he follows. He lowers his head, swishes his tail and gives a little snuffling sigh as we walk along a tree-lined laneway towards his paddock. He looks relaxed, and he trusts me to lead.

It is humbling, somehow, that this mighty animal quietly subjugates his power and his will to mine.

"He thinks I can do this," I say, in wonder.

"Of course." Linc looks at me and frowns a little.

"Training must be a big responsibility." I am thinking of this grey, and of Dash, and those poor war horses I've read about who worked so hard for their soldier riders then were shot, or abandoned overseas to starvation, mistreatment and death.

"It is." Linc's reply is husky, heartfelt.

"We ask the horse to trust us."

"Yes." And as Linc meets my eyes, I'm not sure if we're just talking about horses anymore.

"But that trust can be betrayed." I watch Linc closely, but he just nods and walks on. He seems so genuine and so undisturbed, I can't help but be confused over the disconnect.

Really? But it's not me who's going around kissing people I shouldn't. I don't know what to think about him.

We've reached a gate. I hand the gelding's lead to Linc, and swing the gate open so he can bring the horse in. He gives the grey's crest and neck a brief rub then slides the halter free over his ears. "There you go, mate."

The gelding shakes himself thoroughly and wanders off in the direction of his water trough. He takes a long, slow drink, the apple in his throat bobbing delightfully, his silver mane and dappled hide reflected in the erratic ripples.

I watch the horse, absorbed.

After a time, I look up and catch Linc watching me watching the horse. His look is unmistakable. I write it into my novel every time my coachman looks at Hattie.

I can't believe that after all I've done to him, and more lately to avoid him, he still looks at me like that. I can't believe my reaction either. My belly flips and I am frozen to the spot. Linc doesn't belong to me, but I want to tear off his shirt and have him tear off mine and push me up against the rails. I want his hands against my buttocks and his teeth against my lips, with no space for even a hay wisp between us.

I want him so much, my body aches just thinking about it. *What is wrong with you, Kate?*

I avert my eyes and step back. There is still naked desire in his face but now he is uncertain. He clears his throat. "Kate, I..."

"Linc, don't."

He stops and I feel shock radiating from him. "But I just want to..."

"Don't." I can't forget the sight of Sue coming out of the gallery yesterday, her limp pronounced, her calipers winking in the sun. Linc's assiduousness as he reached over to open the car door. Mira's glowing gaze, in that luxurious hotel. "It doesn't feel right, so don't ask me. I can't."

Linc runs one hand through his hair with a frustrated sigh. For a long, fraught minute, he watches the horse and a silence slides in between us. "I don't understand," he says, at last. "Is it your ex? Do you still love him?"

I feel a surge of anger. "What does Jeffrey have to do with anything?" My flashing gaze meets Linc's and I'm surprised to see confusion in his. *If anyone should be confused around here, it's me. What are you playing at?*

And I wonder if I really know Linc – or myself – at all.

I step out of the paddock, swing the gate shut and stalk off towards the house. I am glad there is no sign of Sue or any other occupant in the majestic old villa as I approach. I travel home with Olive, vowing silently to keep well clear of Lincoln Brady.

That night, I get frenetic. I paint two windowsills in a light cream and my back door bright red without even trying any test pots.

Linc stares after Olive's little car as it skitters down the drive. *What the hell just happened?* He'd thought they were really connecting, but Kate cut him off cold. He didn't even get a chance to show her the old landau in the barn. Kate's coachman would drive something like it, with a high-stepping pair in the shafts.

He returns the halter and ropes to the tack shed, pausing in the quiet gloom. He feels the dull ache of desire, a familiar state for him when Kate is around, but the winking coals are banked by rejection. Her words still sting. What is not 'right' about him? Is she genuinely uninterested?

He recalls that kiss in her kitchen, her body leaning hungrily into his. He could have sworn... What is he missing? What more can he do?

The stable cat jumps up onto the bench beside him. With a guttural, frustrated grunt, Linc reaches out to rub her head with deft fingers. Fixating on Kate's anger today won't help him. He lets his thoughts drift to her fictional coachman and what is obviously a steamy historical romance. No wonder Kate has looked so hot and bothered, every time he's dropped by and she's been writing. It's a pity she is not in such a lather about him.

Still, if she is interested in horse-drawn vehicles, it might be a good prompt to get the landau tidied up. He's been meaning to do it since Mum died. With oiled timber and fresh paint it will look stunning, and he is sure Kate will like it.

Chapter 10

I have kept Lori's car, as she hadn't needed it. In the morning I give it a thorough wash, the interior a quick vacuum and tidy, and drive it round to her house.

When I get to Lori's place, I am shocked to see her in tears. "What's the matter? Are the boys OK?"

Lori clings to me. "The boys are fine, but Nessa has just rung. She found Gus's truck overturned on the road out to their farm. She called an ambulance and they're taking Gus to hospital – I need to go and see him!"

"Of course. Are you OK to drive? Do you want me to come with you?"

"No, can you stay and mind the boys? Keep my car, I'll take the Torino." Lori and I are already moving to the garage, opening the door to reveal Gus's muscle car hunched there like a sleek, orange cat. Lori jumps in. "I don't know how long I'll be, Kate, I'm sorry..."

"Just go!" I yell, and I'm sure I hear the squeal of tyres as she rounds the letterbox and hurtles towards town. I pray we won't have to deal with two road accidents today.

At the sound of the high-performance engine, Taika arrives at the door. He peers past my legs. "Where Mummy gone?" he asks.

I realise I don't know how bad Gus's injuries are, or what Lori wants me to tell the boys. I say cheerily, "Mummy had to go out for a while. Let's go find your brothers and make some lunch."

"We had yunch," says Taika, staring at me with a child's unerring instinct for something wrong. "Where Mummy?" He is joined by Nikau and Tommo, who share the same instinct and are watching me now with large, dark eyes full of concern.

"Daddy had a problem with the truck. Mummy's gone to help him. I'll stay with you until she gets back." I look at the worried faces before me and decide a distraction is needed. "How about we take Penny for a walk to my house? We can make some lemonade."

"Yay! Yemonade!" Nikau is immediately sold on the idea. After a moment's hesitation, his twin goes along with it and they race off to the laundry to get Penny's lead.

Tommo is still unsure. "Mum didn't say goodbye."

"Sorry, darling, Mummy had to rush. She left me in charge, but it will be nice to have an assistant. Can you help me look after your brothers today?"

Tommo looks at me seriously for a moment. "Yes," he says. "I think you'll need it."

In the end, I have the boys to stay overnight. We drop Penny home in the late afternoon, feed her, and leave the back door open so she can access the garden. Lori calls to say that Gus's condition is stable, but he has bruising all over his upper body and his right leg is broken. There appears no other serious damage but they will keep him overnight for surgery and surveillance.

Lori offers to come home. I tell her to stay with Gus. "The boys and I are fine. We are about to go to my house to make bolognese sauce for dinner."

Lori reminds me that it's Rae and Hemi's wedding tomorrow, and we were to help with the setup. I groan audibly, and she begins to apologise so I have to pull myself together and try to sound enthused. Oh, and capable. Lori gives me instructions on clothes for the boys to wear, and I pack a bag for them while she is on the line. She reminds me to throw in their toothbrushes, and good shoes, then we sign off and I head for the door.

I jangle the car keys and yell, "We're go-ing!" And just like that, three boys appear. I am almost tumbled in the scrum as they jostle past, yelling, and run for the car.

Back at Waiata, I sit my nephews together on the big couch in the front room. I tell them that Daddy has had an accident with his truck and his leg is broken. I assure them he will be fine, and explain that Mummy is at the hospital to help look after him.

"My budgie bwoke his yeg," says Taika, helpfully.

"Yep, da budgie died," Nikau nods, in solemn concurrence.

"I broke my wrist and I didn't die. Will Daddy die?" Tommo had been pretty calm until his brothers' revelations.

"No, no, darlings, Daddy will be fine. The doctor will put a big plaster on his leg and then he'll have to hop around on crutches for a few weeks, that's all, while it gets better."

At this, Tommo cheers up and the twins leap, shouting, from the couch. They go hop, hop, hopping along my hallway until my ears are ringing with their noise and the sunset chorus in my garden has scattered in fright. I'll bet there are no birds within a hundred yards of my homestead this evening.

Tommo and I pile fresh herbs and chopped tomatoes into the kitchen blender and make a tasty bolognese sauce. We serve it outdoors, to reduce the amount of cleanup I'll have to do later, along with a big bowl of pasta. The boys are delighted with the novelty of eating spaghetti on my verandah, underneath the roses.

We have an entertaining evening, with a somewhat modified version of the twins' usual bath, storybook, bed routine. Tommo and I eventually manage to get them both showered and read to, and I tuck them in together in the big bed in Sunflower.

I turn the bedroom light off, leaving the bathroom well-lit, down the hall. I listen to the little boys chattering while I sit with Tommo in Bluebell. Tommo climbs into the soft, blue-quilted bed, I curl up in the captain's chair by the window, and we talk for a while in the soft lamplight. Tommo is worried about his father, so we talk about that, then about school, and football, Penny, and Olive's huskies.

Nikau comes out twice for a drink of water, and Taika six times in the space of twenty minutes to 'do wee'. However, they must both eventually surrender to the exhaustion of the day. By the time I wish Tommo goodnight and tiptoe back up the hall, the twins are asleep.

I collapse on the couch, my aching eyes closed, my aching feet propped up on the ragged, velvet arm. This motherhood gig is exhausting. I wonder if I can bother actually going to bed.

I cannot write weddings because I feel so conflicted about my own. So, there will be no weddings in my novel and Hattie is unlikely to have a traditional happy ending. Her marriage is a mess anyway. But in the morning, despite my cynicism about the whole marital thing, I find myself hoping for the best for Rae and Hemi's wedding.

The day dawns cool and overcast but Tommo assures me cloudy skies are good for wedding photography, when he and the twins come bouncing into Rose. It is barely six, and I'm barely awake, but the boys look as fresh as daisies.

"How do you know about wedding photography?" I ask, dragging on a sweatshirt and leggings and heading for the kitchen.

"Youtube." Tommo opens the fridge. He pulls out a bottle of milk, and the twins climb up and tumble three different cereal boxes off the shelf.

"Moosyi. Yuck. Bran fyakes. Yuck. Weetbix. OK." Taika sorts the boxes, discards the muesli and bran cereal, and distributes wheat biscuits to everyone.

"You watch Youtube videos on wedding photography?" I rescue the milk bottle from Nikau's enthusiastic tipping technique, and ensure three bowls of cereal are prepared with minimal spillage.

"Yep. Linc showed me some of Sue's work. Mum says Sue is taking the photos today, too, for Rae."

"Oh." Another string to Sue's bow. Not only is she an accomplished career woman and lives in the midst of immaculate gardens, but she's a wedding photographer, too? "Eat up, boys. I'm going to take a shower."

I stand under hot water until I have restored some semblance of good mood and faith in myself, and get out when I hear a thump and a yell.

Nikau bursts into the bathroom. "Taika broke dat ting in da younge room."

I sigh, wind a towel round my hair and tuck another around my body. I tag after Nikau to discover that Taika has swung on the carved rimu mantelpiece and it has become detached from the wall. There is plaster dust everywhere and torn wallpaper, and three big-eyed, anxious boys are staring at me.

"Good one," I tell Taika. "That mantelpiece has been standing for a hundred years and it's lasted just a few hours with you lot here." Taika bursts into tears so I reach down, wrap him in a hug and say, "Don't worry, I can look up how to fix it later."

"You can look on Youtube," suggests Tommo, helpfully.

Taika brightens. "You can wing Daddy. Or Yinc!"

"No one's ringing Daddy. Or Linc." Especially when I'm wearing only a towel. I confiscate all phones within sight, set up cartoons on my laptop for them to watch, and go and think about clothes.

I have to wear something pretty but practical, because with Lori occupied with Gus I'll have to help with flowers and bunting before the actual event. And I can't guarantee I'll have time to come home and change. I open the wardrobe in Rose, drag out half a dozen dresses and agonise for a while.

At last, I lay out my favourite Audrey Hepburn-style tea dress in dark green. I pair it with silver strappy sandals and Mum's pearls. I don't dress yet because I still have to get the boys ready, so I head down the hall in my towel – and bump straight into Linc.

I gasp and clutch my towel. Then I remember I'm wearing a hair towel as well, and I groan inwardly. *Kate, you must look a fright.* Linc looks surprised, then amused, and we are mobbed by boys before either of us can say a word.

"I use da Skype. I done call Yinc!" Taika shouts.

"Yinc can fix dis ting!" Nikau is nodding enthusiastically.

Tommo looks apologetic. "They did it while I was getting a drink in the kitchen."

"Oh, joy." I look up at Linc. From his expression, he's not sure whether to laugh or run away, but his chocolate eyes betray a wary smile and I know he is not annoyed.

I might be. I'm not sure yet.

Linc holds his palms up. "I'm sorry to barge in. The boys said it was an emergency. I knew Lori and Gus weren't around, so I came straight over."

"It's OK." *The only emergency around here is what I'm wearing.* I decide to play it cool. I unwind my hair towel, toss it through the bathroom door, and shake out my hair. Then I take a firm grip on my other towel, turn Linc around and steer him ahead of me into the lounge. "Come and see what the fuss is about."

I show Linc the mantelpiece disaster, standing well back so he can't get another eyeful of me in my towel. He agrees with the twins that it is totally an emergency and heads out to his ute for some tools. I take the chance to bolt down the hall, slip into my leggings and sweatshirt, and look for the bag containing the boys' wedding clothes.

"Here." I wave the bag at Tommo. "I'm making it your job to supervise your brothers and help me get everyone dressed."

And I'm glad I have his assistance because it is like herding cats.

In the thirty minutes it takes Linc to reattach the mantelpiece, clear out the damaged wallpaper and do an initial repair of the plaster, I manage to get one and a half twins dressed and raise my voice in despair three times.

After I've sent Tommo running after Taika for the fiftieth time, Linc looks over to meet my frazzled gaze. "I've finished all I can for now. How about I mind the boys while you sort yourself out?"

I bristle at the suggestion I need sorting out, then remember it's a wedding I'm going to, and leggings just won't cut it. "Yes. Yes! Give me ten minutes."

Taika comes tearing past in his undies, holding his socks to his nose and trumpeting like an elephant. Linc catches him on the fly and tips his chin at me. "Go, now. Quick. You may not get another offer like this." And he is grinning, and I'm a weak-kneed hot mess at the sight, and I dash down to the Rose room.

He is Sue's, he is Sue's, he is Sue's.

I have my mantra down pat by the time I emerge in my strapless green dress, sandals and pearls. I've styled my hair and applied a little makeup, just enough to make an effort, not too much for an outdoor event. And I think, even for me, I look good.

Linc is playing with the boys when I walk in. He has Nikau in his arms, Taika on his shoulders and Tommo wrapped around his leg. They are all dressed and he is laughing with them, then he looks over and sees me.

His jaw drops. I haven't seen that before, I'd always thought it was a figure of speech, but he looks genuinely stunned at the sight of me. At first I think it's because I forgot to button my dress and I am naked or something. But no. I realise he just likes what he sees.

Twirl, Katie. I listen to my mum, throw caution to the wind, and twirl.

"Wow, auntie Kate," Tommo blurts, "You look like a movie star."

"She does." Linc is still staring in open admiration. He sets the boys down, clears his throat and says, "Righto, I'd best be going home." Taika, Nikau and Tommo clamour at once for a lift in his ute, and Linc looks to me.

I am unaccustomed to the role of parent, but I do my best. "Tommo can go with you. The twins have to sit in special seats so they need to come with me." Over a chorus of groans from the twins, I assure them, "We'll drive right behind Linc. You'll be able to see every drift and burnout."

"Me? Never!" Linc protests but he is smiling. Then a thought seems to strike him. "Is it the way I drive, is that the problem?" He is now talking over the boys' heads, literally and figuratively, and in an instant we are back on shaky ground.

"What?" I stare at him. All our comfortable cooperation in getting the boys ready seems to evaporate. I feel like we're speaking different languages now, and I am confused. "Your driving has nothing to do with anything." *I like the way you drive. It's your cheating I don't like!*

Linc rubs his jaw. He looks about to say something, but Tommo tugs at his shirt and he shrugs. "OK. Come on, Tommo."

And then he is gone. I turn away to find my purse and Lori's keys. I hustle the twins out the door.

In the Kingswood, Tommo bounces about on the wide leather seat, chatting incessantly in his excitement. Linc lets him ramble on while he thinks about Kate. He knows Kate wants to keep him at arm's length, but he is totally frustrated and confused as to why. And he cannot, simply cannot get her out of his head.

It doesn't help that she looks stunning in that dress. And in a towel, for that matter. Linc groans.

"And then auntie Kate said not to call you. Does auntie Kate not like you? Because she really, really didn't want us to call you."

"Your auntie Kate and I are... friends." Linc's voice catches on the word. *Just friends, dammit.* "And perhaps she wasn't ready for visitors."

"Oh." Tommo looks like he hadn't considered that. "Because she was wearing a towel?"

Linc grips the wheel tight. He wants to swing hard right, hit the gas, drive hell for leather back to Kate and kiss that frustratingly gorgeous woman right out of her green dress. Or her towel, or whatever. Definitely her whatever.

"Hmm? Yes, mate. Because she was wearing a towel."

Kate has been pretty damn clear lately that the last thing she wants is for him to make a move on her. So 'friends' it will have to stay. *Damn it.*

Linc has reached his driveway. He swings in, murmurs, "Hi, Mum," to her prancing timber horse, and fishtails the ute a little on the drive up to the villa just to give Tommo a thrill.

As they park in a flurry of ricocheting stones, Sue's gaze meets his from across the lawn. She frowns and he realises she is thinking of her gravel. She'd had it all nicely raked for the wedding.

Oops. Linc grins. *What the hell.* So long as he can still annoy Sue, life is worth living.

Tommo leaps out, and Kate pulls up behind them in Lori's car with the twins.

It's time to get to work.

Chapter 11

I am chagrined to find that I actually like Sue. She is a powerhouse of energy and rather bossy, but this is tempered with such good humour and sense that no one seems to mind being bossed. Even me. At first, Tommo and I don't have a clue how to arrange the floral centrepieces so they look their best, or tie the fabric chair covers, but Sue trains us up in no time. Nessa teaches us how to set out the silverware and soon we are arranging tables like pros.

Taika and Nikau create havoc, chasing Brick under and around the tables, so Sue delegates them to unravel the bunting that Linc is hanging in the garden. This is more hilarious than constructive, but it gets them out of our way. They idolise Linc, so they stick at the task far longer than I'd imagined.

I text Lori a couple of photos of her boys being helpful. Also, one of Taika wrapped so tightly in pink and white bunting that you can see only the top of his head.

Lori sends a thumbs up emoji and asks, 'Can you leave him like that? He'll be a lot less trouble.' When I ask about Gus, she says the hospital staff are happy with his progress and he'll be able to go home this afternoon. I update Tommo, and feel like I can relax a bit.

But not too much. Linc is like a blazing light at the edge of my senses. I am hyper aware of his every movement, every word, every laugh. I know exactly where he is and what he's doing at all times. I have to catch myself from watching him, from responding to him... in a way that's obvious, at least. I can't help what my body does.

At one point, he strips off his shirt to climb a tree and untangle some bunting flags Taika tossed up there. As he swings down, his tanned torso rippling, silver cording gripped between his teeth, I just want to swoon at his feet.

Now you're behaving like Lady Hatwick, Kate.

Linc sets his feet on the grass, sweeps up his shirt and shrugs into it. His gaze passes briefly over mine and I'm afraid he's caught me watching him. I rustle a brief smile and turn back to flower arranging, my heart racing and my cheeks pink. Sue calls him and he heads off across the lawn to fix a problem with the stage, my heart and my eyes following him.

As the afternoon wears into evening, all this heightened, helpless emotion just makes me feel sad.

Weddings are about love. Have you noticed? Hemi and Rae are in love, that much is clear. And I'd hope so because it is their wedding day. And Sue must love Linc, at least in her own way, because I saw one of the bridesmaids eyeing Linc after the ceremony and she asked Sue, "Is he as perfect as he looks?"

"I dunno," Sue replied. "I suppose so. He has flaws alright." Here, she gave an oddly familiar grin. "Sometimes he is too kind for his own good. And no one can say he's the most communicative bloke!" Sue laughed then, and went off to photograph the cutting of the cake, and I had to leave before I burst into tears right in front of the nosy bridesmaid.

I sit now in the dark on the villa's front step, staring hard at the crescent moon until my eyes stop leaking. *Yes, he's too kind. Too kind to me.* And he can communicate alright, just not always with words. I've seen him with his horses. And I've had those sexy, corded arms around me.

But I cannot, ever again.

I can hear Tommo and the twins playing a raucous game with some other kids, in the kitchen garden to my right. They are safe there, Olive is watching them from the farmhouse kitchen while she makes coffee and chats with Derryn. She told me to go and have fun, that she'd watch the little monkeys and take them home to Lori by eleven. But, well...

Fun?

For once, my mother fails me and says nothing in reply. And I don't want to hear anything Jeffrey has to say. I tip my head back and let the ambience of the party wash over me.

The night is absolutely stunning. The huge garden to my left is like a fairy palace, lit by lanterns and candles and filled with beautiful people, from the terraces to the river. Guests have been streaming in and out of the villa all afternoon, all evening, yet the floors are still shining, the foyer immaculate, the table settings fresh and sparkling.

I have to give Sue credit, she is an amazing wedding organiser. And the villa is a stunning venue.

"Bored already?" Linc, carrying bottles of spirits to refresh the bar, has paused behind me in the foyer. He has a slight frown on his face and I feel I am interrupting him.

"Um, no, I was just... watching the moon."

Linc moves as if to join me, but then hesitates as an uproarious chant of "Vod-ka, vod-ka," starts up in the front room. Mira is leading it, I can hear her voice over the rest.

"Li-inc!" she yells from her barstool. "Where's the *booooze?*"

Linc gives a lopsided smile. "If you need alcohol with that, just follow the drunken singing to the bar." I think he will leave now, but he pauses midstep. Perhaps he's seen something in my face. "Are you feeling OK? Should I get Sue, or Olive?"

His enquiring gaze meets mine across the soft-lit foyer and I realise he is just a few timber floorboards away, but it feels like a million miles.

"Yes. No! I'm fine, thankyou, I think I'll go watch the band." I leap to my feet and flee for the rose-bordered terrace before his concerned, brown eyes can set me crying again.

Seriously, Kate, get a grip. Yes, that's Jeffrey, back in my head. I am all dressed up in my pearls, cute dress and heels, and I am drowning in memories – did I tell you I hate weddings? – while I pine for a love I can't have.

The band is a professional covers group hired from Wellington – Hemi wanted his wedding night off – and they have the dance floor surging. I stand for a while to watch, and I can't help being slowly drawn in by the dancers and the rhythm.

Billie, in particular, is in her element. She's outgoing at the best of times, but on a dance floor with a rockin' beat it seems Billie is the life of the party. I can't help but watch her. And so do all the men. She is a bright-haired, svelte, gyrating beauty, dancing and whooping and dragging others up with her until the dance floor is packed with moths enslaved to Billie's flame.

Even Lollie is there, spinning with Mel and Dave, her wheels sparkling with little fairy lights.

I am not immune. Billie soon catches my hand, her eyes alight, and drags me to join her pulsating crowd. I cannot help but laugh with her, and dance with her, and I no longer wonder what Linc sees in her. I let myself become lost in the music. My Audrey Hepburn dress flares out and ripples as I spin and spin and spin...

A few songs in, the rhythm slows to a waltz and someone grabs me. I have a brief jolt of hope that it's Linc, but the hand is sweaty and I realise with surprise that it's Brad. Brad from Real Estate, in a grey suit and shiny, silver tie.

He encloses my hand in his, pulling me closer. "Dance this one with me. I'm sure you can waltz. You look totally like you know how to waltz, you know?"

I wonder if he is drunk. I try to pull away, but he fixes me with big, blue, pleading eyes, "Come on. It's my sister's wedding. Please."

What can I do? I dance with him. And I do know how to waltz, I'm quite good at it, my mother made sure of that. As I twirl round the dance floor, keeping clear of Brad's two left feet, subtly leading without appearing to lead, I see Olive in the crowd watching me, and Linc at the edge of the terrace. His face is in shadow but there is heat in his gaze.

I feel like there is nothing I can do about Brad's arm around me, tonight. Nothing I can do about his beery breath on my cheek, no way to stop him when he insists on holding me tight for the next dance tune. In a reckless, defiant, night-fevered way I don't care to, anyhow. We waltz on, round and round, and in the corner of my eye I see a woman with glossy dark hair dash up to Linc and kiss him on the mouth, right there on the terrace.

I almost miss a step. Yes, definitely. She is hanging off him now, shouting into his ear, and Linc responds with a distracted smile, dragging his eyes from me. She places both hands boldly on his biceps, feels him up, and laughs.

No way! Is that Christa? I am astonished, but Brad has seized the lead in my moment of distraction and he sweeps us away. When I look back, Linc and the woman have gone. When the second waltz ends, I slip from Brad's protesting grip and make straight for Olive.

"Hi, Olive, don't worry about taking the kids home, I'll do it now." Before she can respond I sweep past her, scoop my purse from my long-abandoned chair and wave 'bye' to Rae across the room. Then I scarper.

Tommo is abuzz with stories on our way home in the car. The twins are asleep before I've passed the timber horse at the gate. I turn onto the long, dark highway and try to drag my mind from the terrace, from the sad, quizzical gaze I saw on Linc's face.

Sad? That makes no sense, and I want to cry again. There are holes in my heart tonight the size of my own, long-regretted wedding, and of Jeffrey's sneer, and of Linc's caressing, forbidden hands.

I wonder if I am going mad.

Lori is chirpy, solid and warm when she hugs me, and together we carry the twins inside.

"Goodnight, Tommo," I say, as he climbs into his bed beside the twins' bunk. "Thankyou for all your help today."

I delight in the quick, proud little grin that skips across his sleepy face, and I fill with all the love of an auntie again. My nephews are busy and demanding and I don't know how Lori copes every day, but being here to spend time with them is a blessing.

I'd do well to remember that and stop moping.

I straighten my shoulders as I follow Lori into the kitchen, and we make hot chocolates together at the breakfast bar. As we sip, she asks for gossip. I tell her about the wedding ceremony, Billie's dancing, and Lollie's fairy lights. I omit anything about Linc, or Sue. I ask how Gus is feeling, and Lori says he'll be fine but his leg will be in plaster for at least six weeks.

"He won't be able to drive, but perhaps that's a good thing. He's been working far too hard lately."

I smile. "I think you both have."

Lori sighs. "Oh, I know." She meets my gaze. "Gus and I were talking in the hospital while we waited to leave tonight. This has been a real wake-up call for us. We think we'll make some changes. We'll hire another driver, or sell one of the trucks to make sure Gus gets more time at home."

"That's a great idea! It will be good for all of you."

"Yes." And my beautiful sister's smile crumbles. She leans on my shoulder and says, through her sobs, "When Nessa told me his truck had rolled, I was so, so scared I'd lost him. Oh, Kate! What's the point of all this work, the new house, our gorgeous whanau, if Gus is not here to share it?"

I hug her and whisper soothing words. And for the first time in my life, I think I know a little of how she feels.

Linc wants to hit something. Or someone. Perhaps a certain male someone in a stupid, grey suit with a stupid, silver tie. He's never felt like this before and he knows he must get a grip. Sue will be unimpressed, to say the least, if he starts thumping her guests.

He has to talk to Kate. He excuses himself awkwardly from Christa, but when he gets back to the dance floor, Kate has gone. Bradley is not there either. Linc wades through the crowd by the bar, searching, then does a quick lap of the garden to check all the canoodling couples.

He ends up by the front door, with no sign of Kate or Brad.

Linc's heart is pounding. He feels desperate, but he's unsure what to do next. He stands there and stares at the moon for a long, fraught moment, willing himself to calm down.

"She's gone home." Olive is passing through the foyer with a trayful of coffee mugs. She catches Linc's expression. "Alone. Well, with Lori's boys."

Linc exhales in relief, and Olive studies him with a worried gaze. She steps forward to say something but then suddenly Billie breezes in, all smiles, to commandeer Linc's attention.

"There you are, you sexy man. Rae and Hemi want to leave soon. Bring the car round, will you? There's a darling." Billie pats his cheek lingeringly, graces the air beside him with a scarlet pout, and dashes away.

Linc gives Olive a hectic nod and she rolls her eyes in response. Linc takes the front steps three at a time, and jogs out to the stables. Hemi had wanted to borrow the vintage Rolls but she can be a devil to start. At least this will distract him from going after Bradley. Or Kate.

And it is hard for him to watch Hemi and Rae's delight in each other as they kiss on the front porch, and throw the bouquet. Mira catches it, then catches his eye, so heaven help him now. He keeps his gaze fixed firmly on the sleek saloon car as it drives away.

Linc's love life is a miserable shitfight. He only wants the one woman who doesn't want him.

Chapter 12

On Sundays, Olive opens her shop for just a few hours over lunchtime. I go in with her to lend a hand. For something to do, more than anything. My house seems empty this morning without the boys running through it.

I am drying coffee cups and putting them away, and Olive is wiping a sleek rag over the countertops and windowframes when Linc arrives. He is smiling but there is an edge to his manner and I wonder what's bothering him. I don't imagine it could be me.

And I can't tell from the conversation. He chats with Olive about the horses, updating her on the grey, whose handling under saddle is apparently coming along beautifully. Then he mentions training Dash to harness. I am touched to discover he has begun this, despite the fact that we are barely speaking.

He is distant and polite as I make his coffee, but when I pass it over the counter I'm sure I don't imagine the quick burn in his gaze as his fingers meet mine around the cup. I snatch my hand back in confusion, my cheeks hot.

Linc unfolds his long frame from the café stool and nods to each of us, evenly. "Bye, Kate, thanks for the coffee. Olive, go easy on the red wine tonight, you know how you get after weddings."

"Linc, darling, you know all my secrets." Olive winks, and Linc laughs. He strides away across the courtyard. Olive leans out the window a little further, ostensibly to wipe down the glass.

"How *do* you get after weddings?" I am curious.

"Restless." *Lonely*, perhaps, is the subtext.

I don't want to think about Olive being lonely. It makes me worry that I'll be lonely too, in twenty years' time.

"Are you ogling Linc?" I joke, to distract from my thoughts.

"Of course! He is beautiful, haven't you noticed?" Olive tips her head and grins at me. And I am surprised, but perhaps I shouldn't be. Olive is a much older woman but she is also fun, outrageous and spontaneous. I can see that could be sexy. Hell, I find it sexy in my characters. I wonder, does Linc find Olive sexy?

I think about Linc. He is fun, too, but in a steady, warm way. He is kind and thoughtful. I don't think being outrageous is his style. "Olive, can I ask you a personal question?"

"Of course, blossom."

"Did you and Linc ever have a... thing? He seems to know a lot about you."

Olive laughs and flicks her teatowel at me. "I never kiss and tell, Kate – about the men I caught or the ones who got away. But I *can* tell you something. That man is in love with you, and if you let him go, you're a bloody fool."

"Linc? In love with me? Are you nuts?" I stare at her, the teatowel in my hand forgotten. "The other day I saw him having lunch with Mira! And after talking with you, I think Linc's life may be more adventurous than I'd imagined."

Olive gives a dismissive snort. "And you were dancing with Brad the real estate agent at the wedding last night, what does that mean?"

"That's different. It was his sister's wedding, he asked me to dance and I felt bad to say no." *I couldn't say no.* "It doesn't mean anything."

"My point exactly," says Olive emphatically, and she disappears into her office.

I am left cleaning the coffee machine myself, fuming, and even more in the dark about Linc.

I am still feeling conflicted that evening about the idea that Linc and Olive may have been together – and irritated that I even care – when the familiar burble of Linc's ute disturbs the sunset chorus in my garden, and he pulls up outside.

Damn. What's he doing here? I distractedly stuff my dinner into the sink, drop my water glass in the bin and attempt a haphazard tidying of my hair. I am wearing yellow flannel pyjamas and ugg boots, and can only pray no woman could look better on a Sunday evening, alone in a farmhouse in a paddock.

Looking good, Katie. I hear my mother's voice and smile in spite of myself – then realise what I did to my glass, and rummage in the bin to retrieve it.

"Kate?"

I fish the glass out triumphantly and glance at him, tall, dark and bemused at the back door. "I just, er... I just..." I drop the glass into the kitchen sink with my scrambled dinner and flick my fingers clean under the tap. "Um. Hi."

"Hello." He is still standing on the doorstep. He nods at my bright red, newly painted door. "Nice paintwork. Very... red."

"Yes." I tilt my chin. "It was red yesterday, too."

"I didn't notice."

No, you were too busy looking at me in my towel. "Are you coming in?" I tweak my ponytail tight, rub at my nose and pause uncomfortably, looking at him. I don't know what he's here for and it seems he doesn't either, because he just stares at me.

He clears his throat. "Kate, I don't know how to say this, but it's killing me not to say it so I'm just gonna come straight out with it. I couldn't tell you this afternoon 'cos Olive was there, but last night got me thinking and I..."

"Linc, what are you here for?" I want no reminders of last night. Not of him, or Brad, Christa, Billie, Mira or Sue. I am tired, confused, and short on patience.

He pauses, runs his hand across his stubbled jaw. "Kate." He shifts restlessly on the old porch step, worn smooth by a thousand visitors. "Kate, I really like you. I want to be with you. I want to know if you feel the same about me. Even just a little bit."

"What?" I stare. "I don't understand how you can say that to me. Straight after a wedding, too!" I wonder if he's toying with me, or I've somehow misjudged everything.

Linc looks puzzled. I don't feel like that is a valid expression on the face of a philanderer so I stalk off down the hall, tossing my ponytail in defiance, dredging the fragments of my pride from deep within my battered heart.

Linc follows me in, still in his boots. That's a first for him so it means something, but I can't imagine what. *How dare you say such lovely things to me when I feel so vulnerable, and when you have no right to, anyway?*

I meet Linc in the middle of my lounge room with my eyes blazing. "How dare you?" I snap.

Linc pulls up short, his palms out. "Kate, I'm trying to tell you how much you mean to me!"

"But why say it at all? How can you imagine I want to hear words like that from you?"

"I apologise, I... I'm not very good at this. Maybe it's too much too soon, but I can't help it."

"But what about Christa, last night? She kissed you right in front of everyone!"

"What?" Linc shrugs. "Christa's always like that when she's had a few. She was all over Dave later. Mel clocked her with Mira's bouquet, Mira chased them both with a cake knife, and Dave had to take them all home to sober up."

"Oh." It seems I'd missed the entertainment. "Mira's bouquet?"

"Don't ask."

"Anyway, I saw you having lunch with Mira. You kissed her in the hotel!"

"Mira's brother was my best friend in college. He died. She always has a hard time around his birthday, so I took her out to lunch. We're just friends."

Mira definitely wants to be more than friends. But I realise it's not the right time to say that. Instead, I move up a gear. "Then what about Billie? She kissed you in the street and you liked it, you didn't push her away or anything."

Linc's humour is irrepressible. I catch an invisible subtext bubbling up here, even in the middle of our argument. *Would you push Billie away if she kissed you? You have to admit she's pretty fabulous...*

I glare at him. Linc rubs the back of his neck. "Have you been following me around everywhere, just to catch women kissing me like this?"

"This is not about me." I feel exhausted, strung out, but I need to sort this.

"Alright. About Billie... We had a brief thing a few years ago. Billie met a rich A-lister from the movie business and left with him. Now she's back, and wants to take up where we left off. I told her thanks but no thanks, I don't love the idea of being dumped again when she finds someone better."

"Oh... But what about Sue?"

"Sue?" Linc looks confused.

"Sue, the woman you live with, surely you haven't forgotten her already?"

Linc stares at me, then throws his head back and laughs. A deep laugh, an infectious one, the kind of laugh I couldn't help laughing with on a normal day. But this is not normal. I have been shocked, upset, and now I'm angry.

"What is there to laugh at?"

"Kate." Linc reaches out to touch my hand. He is smiling. "Kate, my love, Sue is my sister!"

"Your sister?" I barely register the 'my love' bit in my shock. *His sister?*

"Yeah, she's lived with me since she came back from America last year. Sue had an accident when she was little and has some ongoing health problems. She also has a crazy work schedule, running my father's company. We find it's easier and she gets more rest if I help with the boring stuff – you know, meals, washing, life in general." He shrugs. "We get on well, so it's no hassle."

I feel confused, foolish. "Your *sister*?" I yelp. "All this time I've been stressing out that I'm moving in on someone else's man and you're a total philanderer, with no respect for the woman you live with, and all this time she's your sister?! You should have told me!"

"You have? You were?" Now it's Linc's turn to look shocked. "But you didn't ask."

"That's not the point." I spin and cross the room to stare out the big bay window. The rambling roses are bobbing in a gentle breeze and there is a fantail flittering in and out of a patch of waning sunshine, catching his dinner on the wing.

I calm down a little and listen to myself. "Actually, maybe it *is* the point." I lean my forehead against the glass, and groan. "I've been such an idiot."

"Kate." Linc steps in close. He swings me round, cups my face with his beautiful, warm hands and looks into my eyes with his beautiful, chocolate gaze. "Kate, my love, I've been besotted with you since the day we met. I've had to keep finding excuses to see you. But I'm the idiot for not telling you. I've watched you, worried about you, been ragingly jealous over you... If I'd found a way to say something, maybe we could have cleared this up sooner."

This is the most Linc has said to me in all the time I've known him, but now I just want him to stop talking. I press my fingers to his lips, and he leans into my touch. I look into his eyes and know that I can drown there.

"Just shut up and kiss me," I say. And he does.

Linc is ecstatic, euphoric, still grinning from ear to ear when he walks into the library of the villa. Sue does a double take and puts aside her accounts. Linc's face is glowing in the lamplight and he looks happier than she's seen him in years.

"Where have you been, bro? You look like the cat that got the cream."

"I went to see Kate." Linc sits down in the Chesterfield opposite, gets up again and stalks restlessly to the window.

Sue reaches down to ruffle her dog's ears. "Hear that, Brick? He finally got off his backside and did something, instead of mooning about after her like a lovesick puppy."

"That's a bit harsh." He pauses. "How did you know?"

"You've been so preoccupied recently, I figured something was going on. Then yesterday I met Kate. She seemed so shy, but she just couldn't keep her eyes off you..."

"Really?"

"Then I saw her dancing with Bradley Evans." Sue laughs. "One look at your face and I knew, alright!"

"Bradley needs to sort his own problems before he starts looking around," Linc growls.

Sue's smile gentles. "He's not been back long, give him a chance. Losing his high-flying job in New York was difficult. Perhaps it'll help Brad if he has someone special to think about." At Linc's frown, she laughs again. "So long as it's not Kate Dale, huh? Never mind, I'm guessing she didn't kick you out on your ear tonight."

Not this time. Linc shrugs, but his expression softens. Scraping at his jaw, he does another restless lap of the room then walks out. In a moment, Sue hears the back door slam.

All good, the horses will settle him. She pokes Brick lightly with her foot. "Pray for Linc, old boy, I think he'll need some help. He's fallen hard for this one."

Chapter 13

I wake in the Rose room at dawn. I trace the petals on the wallpaper and the blonde timber trim around the ensuite door with my eyes, while I daydream in my cool, silent house. It takes me some time to sort through all I have learned and felt in the past few days. I alternate between shock, anger, amazement and delight. I feel a trickling shiver of anticipation when I get to the bit about Linc coming back today.

At that thought, I leap out of bed, tote a fresh sundress and fluffy towel into the big bathroom and take a long, luxurious shower to wash my hair. Afterwards, I take coffee and croissants onto the front verandah for breakfast and spend the morning trying to write.

I don't get much done. I am in a champagne-bubbly glow of delight and anticipation. I relive our conversation the previous evening, his electric kiss, and imagine what it will be like to meet him now with nothing between us, no betrayal of trust or fear of philandering. I can't believe it was never real anyway, that this misunderstanding has held us back for so long.

Oh, Katie. I imagine my mother shaking her head and smiling. She always said I think about things too much.

That prompts me to wonder if Mum would have liked Linc. I decide that she would. Mum was an impulsive person, passionate and mercurial, who lived life to the full. She had been taken in by Jeffrey at first, just like I had been, but she'd turned on him with a vengeance when she'd realised what was going on. It had only taken me too long to catch up. Mum loved a laugh, loved attractive or vibrant people, loved straight, upfront talking, and loved her animals. So, she'd love Linc.

At about lunchtime, Linc's ute burbles up to the Waiata gate. I meet him at the open French doors. He leaps the couple of steps to the verandah in one long stride and catches me up in his arms.

"I've missed you," he says.

"Really?"

"Yes. My grey horse and Dash say hello."

"You must give that horse a name soon."

"Mmm." He closes in to kiss me. "Maybe you can name him."

I lean back to look at him. "Do you really like me?" It still seems incredible.

"Yes," Linc says.

"And you're not cheating on your sister?"

That sounds ridiculous and gets the reaction it deserves. Linc gives me a long look with a raised eyebrow. "No," he says at last. "But now I know what you've been thinking, it explains a lot."

"I suppose it does." I feel deflated thinking of all the times I've pulled away from him, and that day I kicked him out of the house... *Think how much time we've wasted.*

Linc is studying me. "Now we've got all that sorted out, do you think we can start again?"

"We can try." I can't help smiling. I just want to hold him. Linc must feel the same because he pulls me close and his body fits mine tight and hard, like a jigsaw piece I didn't know I was missing.

We kiss, and he traces my face with slow, gentle hands. I feel that Linc is taking care not to go too fast, and I am deeply grateful. My body is responsive to him, it always has been, but my mind is another matter. I am a little nervous. I haven't done this in a long time.

We move from the lounge room to the hall, kissing along its length, and end up in the Sunflower room. I pause in the middle of the room to slip off my heels and Linc catches my hair in his hands, sliding his fingers through it. He smiles as I straighten up and turn to him. I rub my cheek along his hand, dropping tiny kisses along his arm, in the crook of his elbow, the curve of his bicep, nudge my nose under his sleeve to lick salt from his skin.

Linc has goosebumps where I've touched him and I feel a glow gathering inside me. I know this man is just as turned on as I am. I know how much he wants this.

Linc runs his hands down my back now, gathering me close, tightening those biceps until I am snugly pinned against him. I reciprocate by slipping my fingers under his shirt and slowly, tantalisingly sliding his tee upwards, my fingertips tracing his spine and his shoulder blades as I ease the shirt higher and he finally shrugs out of it.

His skin is olive in the shadowed room, his beautiful body lean and muscled, his skin weathered and darker where he's been years in the sun. I lean back to look at him and he grins, bending down to rest his nose and forehead against mine. We are close, the room is quiet and I feel, oddly, like this is a calm before a storm.

I unwrap my chiffon scarf from my throat and Linc's hands travel down my dress, unbuttoning the front. I feel my skin shiver, and butterflies trace his touch. He slides his fingers under the light cotton and runs them up my body, trailing heat across my belly, my ribs, around the swell of one breast. His thumb brushes over my nipple and fire alights there. He leans down to kiss my throat and his shadow crosses my face, cast by the light in the window. I feel a shiver of anxiety then, and it shocks me.

Is it because I haven't done this in so long? Is it because the last time, Jeffrey was so...

I shy away from that thought, and Linc catches my hesitation. I decide to move through it and reach down quickly to cup his crotch. Through the denim I tease him, press against him, and in a moment he responds. He leans into me. As I wrap one leg about him, Linc lifts me neatly, strongly, and slides me onto the bed.

With Linc's lean frame alongside me I feel taller, slimmer, stretched out and weightless against the linen sheets. My dress is open, I am almost naked before him but Linc takes a moment to run his fingers down my profile, my nose, lips and throat, to explore my collarbone and the curve of my breast. His expression is gentle, his eyes smiling, and I am willing myself to be still, to enjoy this and savour the moment. There is dappled light on the ceiling, a lemon tree outside the window and I am trying to lose myself in Linc but Jeffrey haunts me.

As Linc's hand travels along my breast and his mouth follows, his touch more hungry and urgent, I remember other hands. Hands which have squeezed, cruelly. I recall another mouth, which has bitten and sneered. Linc's hand brushes my left shoulder and embraces it, and I feel the twinge of an old scar there.

I flinch in spite of myself, and push my hand reflexively against his chest.

Linc pulls back and studies me. "Kate?"

"Um." I don't know what to say. I want him to keep touching me but there is a voice niggling in my mind, a tiny part of me which is terrified. I try to hide it but it must show on my face.

"Jeeze, what has he done to you?" Linc's eyes slide from dark desire into deep concern. He slips his hand from under my dress and sits up, one hand propping himself on the bed, the other scrubbing at his jaw. It is a familiar gesture, and I know it means he is thinking.

His voice is husky. "We don't have to do anything now, we can just..."

"Linc, I want to but I..."

"Hell, Kate, I'm not really thinking straight right now but even *I* can see that you're not ready." He gives me a rueful grin and flops down to lie alongside me. We both stare at the ceiling for a while, then I slide the folds of my cotton dress back over my body and give a long, slow sigh.

Linc places his warm hand over mine. He rolls to face me and tucks his nose against my shoulder. We breathe together in companionable silence. Linc doesn't seem to feel the need to talk, and I don't know what to say. I watch the ceiling shadows change with the slow march through the afternoon. He closes his eyes, relaxes, and falls asleep beside me.

Linc, I'm sorry. Jeffrey, how much do I hate you? Let me count the ways...

Linc is his usual, easygoing self when he wakes. He kisses me on the top of my head, slides into his jeans and pads down the dusklit hallway to raid the fridge.

I follow him in barefeet, my sundress buttons askew.

"You look like you need sustenance." Linc grins. "What do you have that I can make for you?"

"Not a clue, really, it's been that kind of week." I join him in his inspection of the open fridge. "Look, here is some leftover casserole, feel like heating that up?"

Linc doesn't answer but he reaches for the heavy ceramic dish, scrapes the contents into a saucepan and lights the gas stove. I perch on a stool beside the heavy, old kitchen dresser and enjoy the sight of this lean, handsome man working in my kitchen.

"I'm sorry about today..." I start to say, but Linc waggles his wooden spoon at me and I get thick, rich tomato sauce on the end of my nose.

"If you apologise, I shall serve you cold dinner." But there is a twinkle in his eye and I shake my head, grinning.

I will myself to stay in the moment and put our problem aside for later. I lick the sauce off my nose with my tongue. He follows the movement with his eyes and catches my mouth with his before I can finish.

"Mmm." I have to admit he tastes better than the food.

Linc steps back, observing my blissed-out expression. "I think I'll have to drip casserole on you more often."

"It's a unique approach but it has merit. I wonder if Lady Hatwick would like it?"

"Did they have casserole dishes in her day?"

"I think they had stewpots. The cooking of casseroles is as old as time, I expect. But Hattie doesn't cook, she has people to do that."

"Kind of like you do, today."

"Absolutely. Keep it up. I can see why Sue chooses to live with you." I am smiling, but I feel a little flutter of nervousness at the thought that I'll have to meet Sue properly, someday soon.

I decide I won't follow that line of thought. I push aside the pile of papers and my laptop on the dining table, set two places with floral placemats and cutlery, and let Linc lead us through a quiet, blissfully easy evening together. We eat, he washes the dishes and I put them away, then we curl up on my unsprung old sofa and snuggle, kiss, and watch fireflies blinking outside the night-filled bay windows.

At last, into a long silence, Linc says, "What do you want from me, Kate, going forward?" His tone is kind but a little formal. I have known this must be coming but I still don't have an answer for him.

"I don't know." I try to blink away the tears which, stupidly, crazily, threaten to smother me.

Linc hears the thickness in my voice, perhaps senses how lost I feel about this, and wraps his arm tighter around me. "How about this for an idea," he says. "I'll come round whenever you want me. But I won't ask anything more than this." He gestures to the two of us, cuddled on the sofa. "You will have to tell me when you want things to change."

I twist in his arms and look at him. He seems genuine, he doesn't sound resentful and I don't think he is making fun of me... But I'm not sure I believe it. *How can he be so calm about this? How long would he wait for me?*

My doubt must show in my eyes because he touches the tip of his index finger to my nose and says, "I've waited for you a while already, what's a few more weeks or months?"

"How about years... or decades?"

Linc gives a deep chuckle. "That might be pushing it. But I'll give it a shot."

I tuck my head under his chin and snuggle deeper, as if hiding here will solve all my problems. For tonight, at least. And perhaps it does.

Linc sleeps over with me in Lavender. I lie alongside him, watching the slow rise and fall of his chest, the soft brush of his eyelids, the taper of his nose and jaw in the moonlight. The Lavender room has light, lace curtains which stir in the breeze from an open window, and I imagine those same curtains ruffling in Hattie's room. Would she feel like this, if she were allowed to sleep all night beside her coachman? Would she feel as warm, as safe, as happy? As hopeful?

I wonder if I need to find Hattie a way to do that. Or if her stables romance will be temporary, like her other infatuations, and she will go on bouncing from one frenzied clutch to another. At one stage, I would have thought that writing the latter would be more fun. That a truly steady, supportive, satisfying love was for other people, not for Lady Hatwick and I. Now, I am not so sure.

Linc unfolds himself from my bed early the next morning, eases into his shirt and jeans and heads for the kitchen. He brings me coffee, kisses me on the top of my head, then leaves for work.

I spend my day with my head full of images of Linc, kissing me, sleeping and breathing beside me. I remember other things I've felt, lying beside a man like that. I remind myself that this is not the same man.

I work through my anger at Jeffrey by creating several searing scenes between Lady Hatwick and her husband. She is furious with him, she resents him, hates the power he wields and the patriarchal control he has over her life. She fluctuates between wanting to throw it all away and run off with her coachman, and being terrified of giving up her privileged life and position.

I go to bed in Bluebell, because it is not so full of musk and memories and I might actually get to sleep.

Chapter 14

Sometime in the middle of the night, my cellphone rings. The ringtone is startling in the still quiet of this sleepy, old house. I roll over and look at the screen. The number is private and I consider leaving it, but then realise it could be my lawyer with something urgent. She is working on London time, I know, making enquiries for me.

"Hallo?" My voice is sleepy, and echoes against Bluebell's cavernous ceiling.

"Fucking hell, Kate, do you know how long I've been trying to get hold of you?" Jeffrey's voice slams through me like a tornado and I gasp, stifling a small scream. "I thought you'd vanished off the face of the earth."

I feel frozen. *How did you get my number? Do you know where I am?* My lovely, rambling farmhouse suddenly feels like a trap. I am breathing fast, frightened, my heart hammering. I try to remind myself he is in London, not at my back door.

"Kate? Kate, are you there?" Jeffrey is insistent. "I need to speak with you. Fuck knows it's been a while. I don't know why you don't answer my emails."

You never speak with me, just at me, I think, dully. *And I've blocked you, you bastard*. But my fear is like ice in my veins and I cannot move, cannot hang up on him. I wait, just concentrating on breathing.

"Look, Kate, I know we didn't leave on the best terms and you seem determined to freeze me out – but I've got into a bit of a bind, here. Business is booming, the sky's the limit for my new company but the regulators are sniffing round and I have to come up with some ready money, fast. I heard your mum died and I know she was loaded. Do you think you could lend me some dosh?"

I find my voice. "Me? Lend you money?"

"Well, who else, darling?" His tone has changed now, wheedling, persuasive. "You should *want* to assist me. Especially given that you're my *wife*." He spits the word, then wrests control of his voice again. I can hear the effort it takes him. "Darling, you have a vested interest in my company doing well, so how about it? Do it just for me. I'll text you my account details." He pauses. "Kate, come on. This is a New Zealand phone number, isn't it? I can't imagine you've mastered internet banking but if you have, you can transfer it straight from your bank to mine."

I am hardly breathing as he talks, struggling to hold the phone up, my body and mind feeling limp and battered, useless, helpless. *He knows I'm in New Zealand. He's got my cellphone number. Does he know where Lori lives?* Then the terrifying thought, *What if he comes here to find me?*

If he learns anything about Linc and I, there will be big trouble.

Every bone in my body screams against giving Jeffrey anything, but I have an overwhelming urge to give him everything. To pacify him. To make him go away. Perhaps I will never hear from him again if I give him what he wants.

I realise it has always been this way, with Jeffrey.

He is still talking. "Actually, you won't know how to do it and you'll fuck it up, so I'll call you again when the banks are open and talk you through it. God knows I don't need the hassle. I've got to go now. Make sure you answer the bloody phone, Kate." And with that, he cuts the call.

I realise I haven't agreed to anything. I've barely said anything at all.

I stare at the phone. I am still shaking. I mentally travel over my body and take stock. Heart? Battered. Mind? Still reeling, and I hate myself for answering that call. Muscles? Feel like liquid, but are slowly recovering. I pause. Ears? In shock from hearing Jeffrey's voice after three long years.

And I can't seem to shake it. I hear his voice, his words repeated ad nauseum through all the long hours until dawn. I am feeling haggard and bleak by morning.

Olive looks at me strangely when I tumble into her car in the morning, still pulling on my Doc Martens and buttoning my floral rayon shirt. She opens her mouth to say something, and I raise one finger in the air between us and shake my head.

Don't go there, please.

Olive shuts her mouth with a snap, gives her car a little pat and me a smile, and lurches off down the driveway. Within a minute she is chattering away about her cat's latest scrap with a feral cat who lives by the stream, and the vegan chicken-style pieces she cooked last night. I let it all wash over me, eyes shut, my mind adrift in a fog.

Olive helps me set up for coffees, then asks if I'll be alright while she leaves the shop for half an hour on an errand. I nod, relieved to be alone again. I feel like I can handle the mindless social banter of making and selling coffees today, but I am not ready for anything more complex.

I am terrified. I am waiting for Jeffrey's call.

Billie comes early and orders three coffees, for herself and her sisters. She sits at the open window like a flamboyant sunbird, chattering and laughing, her feathers shining in the sun. I answer her questions on autopilot, and smile, and I imagine she thinks I'm a halfwit but I can't muster the energy to care.

Christa arrives later for her office order, and I don't even hate her today. All I can think is that my phone hasn't rung yet. *It hasn't rung!* I am a shattered, nervous wreck.

Mid-morning, Linc turns up. He slides onto his usual bench stool with a warm smile. "Hey, beautiful." His voice is like his eyes, chocolate and warm, and it brings a tickle to my stomach. But I don't, I won't, I can't. *I'm so sorry.*

I glance at him, slide away from his gaze, and keep my head down as I set about pouring his usual coffee.

Linc gives me a long, careful look. "Kate, what's going on?"

I'm afraid to answer. I've walled up the fear and stress of Jeffrey's call behind bricks and gates of steel, but these few words from him are washing them away, triggering a rush of tears. I feel them hot behind my eyes. I stare blindly at the coffee machine until I can push them down, under control.

"I can see you're not OK. What's wrong?" I am silent, unable to reply, and he asks, "Is it something I did? Please tell me, maybe I can help."

"Um." I clear my throat fiercely and try again. "No... No, I don't think so. Thankyou."

No one can help me. Not you, not Lori, not Olive. Jeffrey knows my cellphone number. If he finds out I love you, heaven help me. And if he finds out where I'm living, I'll need to move far away. I am struck by another thought. *Then I'll never see you again.*

Linc's eyes are puzzled and clouded with worry. I dare not look too closely. I want to climb into his lap and cry into his shirt, and hear him say 'ssh, ssh' again and stroke my hair, but that would be stupid. I will be just stupid Kate again, useless, know-nothing Kate. Kate who is not even divorced and is shackled to a monster.

I try to catch these worthless thoughts and reject them as they slide into view, but I feel so, so tired today. I need him to go away.

I clear my throat. "Linc, I need you to go away. To leave me alone. I can't do this... this... *us.*"

"What?" The hurt in his eyes hits me like a fist. "But after these last few days, I thought..." His voice catches, mid-sentence. I stare down at his hands resting flat on the bench, the blunt nails chipped from hard work. He rolls them over, palms out, and I know he is pleading. "Kate, I meant everything I said. Everything I... we did."

And I know it. Because he pours so much love in, every time he touches me with those beautiful, gentle hands. But

Jeffrey is dangerous and I'm a disaster, and I need Linc to go away.

"I'm sorry," I say, in a small, small voice. I pass him his coffee, give him a tiny smile, and go away to hide in Olive's office until he leaves.

He does at last, but with a long, puzzled glance back as he walks across the courtyard, his lean frame casting a long shadow in the morning light. I slide out round the office door and climb into the soft pile of cushions in the Children's Reading Corner. I curl up there, half-comatose, staring at the ceiling and hearing Jeffrey's voice in my head, until Olive arrives back.

She is talking before she even gets in the door. "Apparently I'm to give you the day off, Kate, starting now, so let's lock up here and I'll take you home."

I stir, and blink at her. "Pardon?"

Olive casts about the room and locates me in the nest of cushions. "Oh. Hello, there. I told him I thought you looked odd this morning, and it seems we were both right."

"I'm OK." I sit straighter, pulling my ponytail tight and smoothing down my clothes. "Really, I am," I lie. I pause. "*Who* was right?"

"I was. And Linc. He stopped me in the street just now and said I needed to give you the day off, that I'm to take you home and ask Lori to drop in on you this afternoon." Olive fixes me with her shrewd, grey blue gaze. "Linc looked worried. What did you say to him?"

"Nothing." I want to cry. I've cut Linc cold, and he is still trying to help me. I don't know whether to be grateful or annoyed. I settle for frowning instead. "Linc should stop trying to rescue me."

Olive raises her eyebrows. I roll to my feet and march ahead of her, down to the coffee machine. I can see several of our usual customers coming across the courtyard, but before I can muster a smiley face to greet them, Olive snaps the serving window closed.

"Sorry, I have to close for half an hour," she sings out. "Come back then!"

"Olive!" I protest, but she grasps my elbow and steers me firmly out the back door, scooping my bag from the office desk as we pass.

"No, you are going home. Linc has bothered to come and tell me something's wrong, so I'll trust his judgement on it. Anyway, you're a wee bit of a thing and you look peaky, a day off will be good for you."

I almost laugh to hear myself described as 'a wee bit of a thing', as I can imagine what Jeffrey would say. But I let Olive steer me out to her car. I buckle my seatbelt and close my eyes while she careens through town, hits the highway, and rockets out to the farm.

Olive decants me solicitously into my farmhouse. "Rest up, dear friend. I won't ask more because it seems you don't want to talk, but I will pop by tomorrow and see how you feel. No pressure to come in, my coffee shop can survive well enough without you!" She gives me a huge, spontaneous hug, then rushes out, leaps into her car and dashes off down the driveway.

I trail my fingers along the timber panelling as I pass down the hall – avoiding Bluebell – fall into bed in Sunflower and sleep for a solid, dreamless hour.

When I wake it is almost lunchtime. My phone is silent, and I can't face checking for calls while I've been asleep. *What if Jeffrey has called me again? Would I call him back?* The day is grey and fitful, the sun pale and weak. I listlessly prepare a peanut butter sandwich, take it into the orchard with a mug of green tea, and eat while lying under the pear tree.

The rustle of twisted branches, warble of birds and flippant dance of leaves rejuvenates me, and I feel grateful for these lovely things. These simple things. These things which have nothing to do with Jeffrey, or corporate investigations, or Linc.

I think about Hattie and the tumultuous life she leads. I wonder how she copes, and I decide she is more extroverted than me. Her outlets for relaxation are socialising, and sex. I potter inside and lose myself in Hattie's life for the afternoon as a way of avoiding mine.

Today, I send Lady Hatwick back to visit her friend, the Duchess of Devonshire, in one of her uncommon residencies at Chatsworth House. Here, Hattie can rekindle her burgeoning romance with the coachman. Yet she finds that maintaining a covert relationship with her coachman is easier dreamed of than done. She is convinced that the Duchess of Devonshire suspects something. While the Duchess is a thoroughly modern woman, there must be limits to her hospitality; Hattie imagines this may include sharing her coachman with her young, attractive guest.

Clandestine meetings are possible – in an empty stable, in a forest covey and, on one memorable night, in a coach partway down a darkened lane. Hattie is on her way home from a ball when Thomas stops the horses, climbs down from his seat and tells the footmen to turn their backs. The two young men stand some distance away in the dark lane, their ears burning, as Thomas opens the coach door and is hauled inside by a lustful, delighted Hattie. These passionate, frenzied clinches involve plenty of rampant bodice ripping, licking of nipples and manly thrusting and they leave my heroine sated, but soon panting for more.

Perhaps me, too, in an odd, ill-defined desperation. In reality, my love life is a self-inflicted desert. After Jeffrey's call, I have rejected Linc, caged my heart, and I feel like swearing off men forever. It's just a shame my body hasn't got the memo.

In the morning, I slide into Olive's little car without a word, and we careen into town and set up the shop as though yesterday never happened. Jeffrey has still not called, and I am full of hope. Brad soon appears, wearing a blue shirt in a kind of shiny material. It seems to make him hot because he's sweating, but he orders a coffee anyway. I place it before him, endure some smalltalk and wait for him to leave. He doesn't.

Brad is blonde-haired and of solid build, taller than I recall from the wedding, with those sapphire blue eyes which are disconcertingly fixed on me. He wants to talk about London.

"I heard you grew up there."

I don't ask where he heard it, but the Carlisle sisters are my prime suspects. Probably not Linc, he doesn't talk much at the best of times. And I don't want to talk about London because, although I may have grown up there, it's also where I met Jeffrey and I'm feeling very sensitive about that right now.

Also, damn it, if Jeffrey's scandalous legal woes multiply I may be mentioned in the London papers. *I'd hate that.* Seriously, I do not want to talk about London.

Brad is polite but determined. He perseveres with his one-sided conversation on all things Britannia for a while, and I stonewall him with equal politeness. At last, he arms himself with a second coffee and trots off to do real estate stuff. I breathe a sigh of relief and hope he is going to gift the coffee to Christa.

The day is fairly quiet, and I see Linc only from a distance. He pulls up outside the feed store mid-afternoon and starts loading bags into his ute. As I watch him, Billie calls my name, dashing across for her coffees, and he glances over. It's a reflex gesture, but now he knows I'm here – he avoids making eye contact and I am too ashamed to seek it. He looks tired and his mouth is a grim line. He seems so unlike his usual, smiling self that my heart bleeds for him.

When the vehicle is loaded, Linc slides into his seat and shuts the door. He sits a moment in the shadowed cab, running his hands over the wheel, and for a brief, crazy, reckless moment I hope he'll get out and come over to see me. But then he starts up the old girl and drives away, his profile resolute in silhouette.

I know. I'm so sorry Linc, I've hurt you. And you can't understand why.

I cannot imagine what encouragement Brad inferred from our last meeting, but he turns up again on Friday morning. I am keeping my head down, trying to get my work done, and I ignore him but he has something to say. It takes him a bit to get around to it, with a lot of waffling about London and New

York, but then he says in a rush, "Will you come with me to the open mike tonight?"

"Pardon?" I stare at him, aghast.

He grins, tugging at his tie. "It's at the Hall. I lost my usual date and I'd like you to come with me, I think it will be fun."

Fun is the last thing I want. I am still raw, battered and sensitive after Jeffrey's phone call. I am desperately trying to avoid Linc, and he might be at the open mike. And how will I manage to link up Hattie's sex scenes, and get her coachman's kit off in their searing, scorching lovemaking if I can't get enough time to write?

"Why don't you take Christa?" I ask, casting about for a distraction.

"Huh?" Now it is Brad's turn to look astonished. "But I want to go with you."

"Um... I don't think it's a good idea." The words sound small and strangled, and I curse myself for being unable to muster something better.

"Why? Is there someone else?" Brad looks a little cross, and I frown reflexively.

"No."

"Then how about it? I'll pick you up at seven."

There are warning bells jangling everywhere for me. I don't even know Brad very well – but he looks so hopeful, so expectant, and I feel so tired and lost I am unable to think of a reason. I say what I can to make him go away, then bustle off as if I'm very busy.

I hide in Olive's office again. "Is he gone?" I ask Olive, when she wanders in.

"Who?"

"Brad. From Real Estate. You know, with the shiny shirts."

"Oh, that Brad. Yes, he's gone." She looks at me with curiosity. "You're looking very odd. Are you hiding from him?"

I lean against the doorframe and sigh. "Yes, I'm hiding. He asked me to go to the open mike with him tonight."

"Interesting." Olive eyes me speculatively. "What did you say?"

"I said yes. I don't know why I said yes, but I did."

"This is the open mike at the Hall, which Linc and his friends will probably be at?"

"Is there any other kind?" I've not said anything to Olive about Linc, but she always seems to know everything, anyway.

"No. And... you don't know why you said yes." This is a statement from Olive, not a question.

"Yes." I shrug. *Because I'm not good at saying no, when I'm feeling like this. When I'm not... strong. You wonder why? Where would I begin?*

Katie, darling, stop being a victim.

"But what about Linc?" Olive is determined to stay on topic.

"What has he got to do with it?" I blush, then frown, then glance away. *I told him to go away and I think I've really hurt him, and now I can't fix it. I don't even know where to start.*

Now it's Olive's turn to sigh. "Kate, remind me to give you some lessons in assertiveness. If you were a horse, I'd graze you on the side of a busy road and take you to pony club and down Main Street every day until you stopped being terrified of everything."

"It's lucky I'm not a horse, then!" My reply is flippant and light as I flounce off to the coffee machine, but for some reason her words have hurt. I had thought I was healing. A phone call from Jeffrey has taken me back three years. *Am I really that hopeless?*

Chapter 15

My evening starts bad and rolls into worse. Brad comes late to pick me up, then tries to blame me for giving him the wrong address. I point out that the homestead name is not only on the front gate of the farm, but on the local street sign as well, because it is an historic site of interest. He is huffy and embarrassed, and we drive in silence to the Hall.

As we step out of the car, I can hear guitars tuning up inside and the familiar rumble of Lincoln's bass. I almost turn and run, right then. But Brad has his hand on my arm, steering me inside, so I go in with him, my heart hammering.

All the Blues Club gang is there. Mira raises a perfect eyebrow as I walk in, trying to look relaxed my 50's-style polkadot skirt, necktie, and chunky heels. Rae cheers, and Mel leaps up from their table to sweep me into a hug. I lean into her for a moment, grateful for the friendly gesture.

As Brad heads straight for the bar, Lollie rolls over, her wheels flashing strobe-like blue and yellow. "Here's my favourite girl with the flash Pommie accent," she yells. "You look rock 'n roll, baby! Dance with me tonight?"

I twirl with a flourish. "It will be my pleasure, Lollie."

"Hear that, you lot?" Lollie yells towards the stage. "Young Kate here wants to dance with me, so stop mucking about and play something really rockin'!"

At the sound of my name, Linc starts up like he's been stung. His eyes meet mine in an instant, over the head of his bass guitar. His gaze flicks to my right, where I know Brad is standing impatiently, holding two drinks from the bar. A fleeting look of despair mars his expression, but then he nods coolly, and turns to speak with Ira.

I honestly don't know what the band plays for the next two sets. I dance with Lollie and Mel, and I'm wrestled around the floor by Brad a few times, but my heart isn't in any of it and my smile is false and tight. Any time a cellphone rings I jump, thinking it is Jeffrey, and my whole heart and soul is up on that stage, intertwined with Linc.

If Linc looks my way, I feel it. Whenever he moves, he catches my eye. If he changes the bass rhythm, I hear it, and my spirit soars while my heart is breaking into pieces before him on the dancefloor.

Brad isn't helping things. He is laughing too loudly and holding me too tight, and I am alarmed at the amount he is drinking. During the third set, when he sculls his umpteenth glass and tries to steer me back to the bar, I pull back and shake my head.

"No, thanks, I've had enough. Also, are you not driving me home?" I smile to soften the rebuke, but Brad bristles.

"Are you saying you want to go already?"

"I'm just saying it'll be more fun if we pace our drinking, and right now you're three sheets to the wind." I'm gritting my teeth, trying to stay polite.

"Dance with me, then." He grasps my hand and squeezes it. "Come on, show me your moves. Your *special* ones."

"No." I resist the urge to stamp on his foot. "Maybe another time. I think I want to go home now." I am nervous, sweating, trying not to panic, hoping that Linc isn't watching me. Watching us. We've fetched up in a dark corner to the side of the band, so probably not.

"What the hell?" Brad leans closer, peering at me through a haze of sweat and alcohol. "Look at Little Miss Uptight here, doesn't know how to have fun. I should take you back to my place and show you some *real* fun." He reaches for me, his gaze intense. I slip sideways and bolt for the nearest door.

There is a Ladies sign over the lintel, so I head straight for the bathrooms. Maybe I can lock myself in one of the stalls until morning, or ring Lori to come and get me.

Brad follows me into the corridor and grabs my hand. "I'm sorry," he says, blurrily, dragging me back. "I didn't mean it. I really like you and I just..."

I spin on my heel, about to give him a piece of my mind, when he lunges forward and kisses me. I back up in the dim light, but Brad is suddenly all over me, his hands clutching at my skirt, his mouth against mine, his body pressing me against the wall. I scream in silence at the memory of another mouth, other hands grabbing and demanding like this, and I realise I can't breathe. *I can't breathe!*

I grapple against Brad, biting down on his lip and pushing him away, but he presses closer. I am gasping, and I feel like my heart has stopped. Brad murmurs in a drunken fervour. He is heavier than me, stronger. In a blind panic, I slide along the wall and grope desperately for something to hit him with. Instead, I find a door handle.

I open it, and the two of us fall through onto the stage.

The band is in the middle of an Allman Brothers classic as Brad and I enter precipitously, stage left. There's an audible gasp from Rae. Brad still has hold of me, and I'm hyperventilating and trying to shake him off, and Linc gets the gist in a microsecond.

He drags his bass guitar over his head, hands it to Rae with a discordant clang, and in three strides he's got Brad by the scruff of his neck. "Let her go, Bradley!"

Brad looks up blearily and protests, "You can't have her, she's mine."

Linc's eyes cut to me and his face darkens. "She's hers." He tightens his grip on Brad and gets up in his face. "Kate doesn't *belong* to anyone. Let her go. Now."

There is something hard in Linc's expression that penetrates even Brad's drink-addled mind, and he releases me. I stumble away, trembling and gasping.

Hemi and Dave sweep in and take charge of Brad. They grab an arm each and steer him off the stage. "Get your head out of your ass, mate, this is the twenty-first century," I hear Dave say as they leave.

Hemi chimes in. "We're taking you home, bro. You need to sober up."

I reel across the rear of the stage and feel Linc's steadying hand at my back. I hear him say, "Rae, ring Lori. Ask her to meet us at Waiata in twenty minutes." He guides me through a door to the right and it takes us straight outside.

I am whimpering with fear, dry retching, struggling not to cry. I lean against a bollard under the streetlights and try to breathe. I feel distressed, angry, mortified. Linc moves up alongside me. He does not touch me but he clicks his tongue, perhaps in exasperation at what's happened, perhaps to soothe. I can't help it. I lean in with a stifled moan and bury my face in his chest. My panicked heartbeat meets his slow, patient one and forms a new rhythm.

Linc goes still a moment. Then he holds me lightly and strokes my hair. "It's alright, Kate, he's gone now, he can't hurt you." His voice is husky and kind. And he's right, in a way.

But you don't know, I want to say. *Jeffrey is not gone. He rang me the other day.*

Linc and I drive home in silence. I am curled up on the bench seat with my head on his rolled-up jacket, and he is driving with his knuckles white, his expression grim. He makes the ute engine snarl, and kicks the back out a little on corners. At the homestead, he hands me over to Lori, gives her a quick précis of the incident and does a sweep of the house, checking the doors are locked, turning lights and heaters on.

Lori turns to me in the hall. "Did he manage to...?"

"No. He grabbed me, he kissed me, we fell through a doorway then Linc dragged him off me."

Lori raises her eyebrows. "Do you want to report this to the police?"

"No," I sigh. I am exhausted. I just want to shower, then sleep.

"You probably should, you know, but we can talk about that later." Lori hustles me into the ensuite of the Rose room. She finds me a fluffy towel, one of my oversized pyjama shirts and new soap. She fusses until I flick water at her and she finally leaves the room.

When I emerge at last, feeling a whole lot cleaner and more relaxed, Lori hands me a mug of hot chocolate. She clinks it against her own. "Cheers, darling. All men are bastards."

I grimace. "I'll drink to that."

Lori grins. "Except perhaps my gorgeous husband, on a good day, and Linc because he made the hot chocolate." Her eyes twinkle and I can't help but smile back. I think again how blessed I am that I found my sister, that I am not entirely alone now Mum has passed. And I'm surprised but grateful that Linc is still here.

Thinking of Mum makes me tear up, and Lori clucks and tucks me into bed. She leaves the Rose room, half-closing the door, and I nestle deep into the soft pillows. Somewhere down the hall, I hear Lori speaking quietly with Linc.

I feel safe, protected, I know I can trust them. I let myself slide into sleep.

At dawn, I wake and sense that the house is empty. Lori has gone home to tend her family. I pad barefoot out to the kitchen and find she has left me a cheery note and a plate of sliced fruit on the table. There are croissants wrapped in a striped tea towel. I turn on the tap to fill the kettle, and hear a car door creak open outside.

I freeze. I lean over the sink and look out towards the Waiata gate. Linc's ute is still parked outside. The passenger door is open. Linc is unfurling his tall frame from the bench seat, stepping out into the early morning sunshine, stretching. My heart bump starts again and I feel overwhelming relief.

I pause a moment at the sight of his shirt riding up over his abs, then unlatch the window. "Are you going to stand about there all day looking decorative, or come in for breakfast?" My voice sounds hoarse from sleep and crying, but Linc flashes a grin at me. I finish filling the kettle, put it on to boil, and hear his boots on the back porch.

I meet him in the hall. "You slept in your car?"

Linc shrugs. "Just in case." *In case Brad turned up overnight.* The words are unsaid, but they hang between us. "Although Hemi is going round to see Bradley this morning, so I don't think there'll be any more trouble." There is a dark glitter in Linc's eyes.

The thoughtfulness of Linc and his friends fills me with gratitude. I think of Hemi's looming bulk and quiet strength, and Brad's short, pug-like stature. No, I am sure Brad won't mess with Hemi. The warning will be heeded.

I find my smile again. "I need to thank you."

"You don't."

"At least let me feed you coffee and croissants."

"I won't say no to that."

Linc fills up my kitchen and my heart – did I just say that? – while I warm the croissants and make the coffee. He doesn't talk much, and I don't either, but the atmosphere feels familiar and comfortable. I can't imagine what he thinks of me, inexplicably cutting him cold, going out with someone else, then needing him to rescue me – again.

Useless, useless Kate.

But Jeffrey's voice seems to have less power, now.

Linc stays until he gets a call from Hemi. He listens, says, "Righto, thanks," then slides his cellphone back into the pocket of his jeans.

He looks at me, his expression serious. "You should be all good now, Kate. Bradley has agreed to get help for his drinking, and the guys will keep an eye on him. But please keep your doors locked. Just for a while."

I search his face and see worry, care, watchfulness. I understand that I've hurt him badly. And last night's incident freaked both of us. But as he turns his chocolate gaze from mine, I see a flash of fear.

Fear? What is Linc afraid of?

I cannot ask because I don't have the right to, and Jeffrey's face hangs before me like a sword. I thank Linc again, follow him outside and wave goodbye in silence. I want to tell him about Jeffrey's call, but it is my problem, not his. And I'm about fed up with being a victim.

When I get back inside, my phone rings.

I stand frozen to the spot. I let it ring and ring, and at last open the call.

He is talking even before I say hello. "About time, Kate. Are you at the bank? Fifty thousand will be adequate for now. British pounds, of course. Make sure you calculate the exchange rate properly, I know you've never had a head for figures. Or anything, really. God, your life must be such a mess without me. I can't say I've missed you that much, there's always some comely thing here who – well, you know how it is. Women love me, Kate. I haven't lost it."

I can sense him preening. "I meant to call you earlier, but Mitzi wanted to get away on the yacht for a few days..." I am waiting for it, and soon his old anger rises up. "I must say it was bloody duplicitous of you to cancel your flight that day, Kate, and not follow me here. And why on earth would you go to bloody New Zealand? I thought we'd agreed you were going to apologise and move back in with me..."

With you and... Mitzi?

I let him rant on, justifying his existence and our shattered marriage to himself. As I gather my thoughts and calm my skittering heartbeat, I hear the old Jeffrey, the incurable Jeffrey, the sleek, self-satisfied, arrogant, abusive Jeffrey, in this complaining, disembodied voice on my phone.

I think about what he is saying. I think about the grey horse I met, and his gentle trust in me. About the handcrafted Waiata gate, and my bold, bright red door. My life now is *not* a mess. It is not perfect, but it is a life I'm forging for myself and I am proud of it. I think of Lori and her gorgeous family, the love they show me and the laughter I share with them. I think of Olive, with her chaotic driving, wild frizzy hair and infectious smile. She would never say such things about me.

I think of Linc. Of his mouth when we kiss. Of his quiet, undemanding company when I cry, and of that sweet, sweet moment as Rae sang *Killing Me Softly* beneath the stage lights and Linc's eyes met mine across the room. Chocolate eyes. Warm. Safe. He may once have compared me to a horse, but he would never want to hurt me. In fact, he's spent an inordinate amount of his time saving me.

These people don't treat me like Jeffrey does. Mum didn't, either. And this is Mum's money, and my heart that's broken, and my long, long years wasted with this man.

I begin to feel angry. A tiny flare of fury flickers. It is deep buried, but it soon catches hold and roars up through my veins. I feel my pulse pounding, and I feel white-hot, surging anger.

On impulse, I interrupt him. "Jeffrey?" He stops abruptly, and I steel my courage. "I'm only going to say this once, then I'll change this number so I don't have to speak with you again. Are you listening?"

I can hear his hoarse breathing on the end of the line. He is nervous, I realise with surprise. He must be in real trouble over there.

"I will not send you money, Jeffrey, not now, not ever. My mother would turn in her grave if I gave you a single cent of her legacy, so it's just not happening. You can sort out your troubles some other way."

"What the fuck? Hell no, Kate. You owe me!"

I am shaking now, barely able to hold the phone, but I feel a newfound, steely resolve. "Not a cent, Jeffrey. And if you have anything more to say, you can contact my lawyer."

"That bitch? She's fucking useless. She doesn't pass on any of my emails. I need fifty thousand by next Friday or I'm fucked. And if I go down with this investigation, I'll take you down with me, you two-faced, useless cow..."

As he descends into a seething rant, I kill the call and throw the phone across the room. Then I get up and turn it off so he can't ring back. But I can still hear his voice in my head. Heck,

I can still hear my voice, too. *How did I manage to say all that?* I've never spoken to Jeffrey like that in my life. To anyone, in fact.

I sink down to the floorboards and lean my head against the wall. I feel brave, shattered, shocked. I feel like Jeffrey might fly down here and try to make me give him the money. For the first time, I wonder seriously if he can. I sift desperately back through what he said.

He knows I'm in New Zealand. But he doesn't seem to know why. I feel a flood of relief. *He doesn't know about Lori.* Lori and I only connected in person after Mum died. And I've never told Jeffrey much about my father. If it didn't involve Jeffrey then, really, Jeffrey wasn't interested.

A tiny kernel of hope joins the red-hot kernel of anger that now rests inside my heart.

Chapter 16

Rain settles in that afternoon, and it continues to pour for another three days straight. I take the weather as a sign to stay holed up inside, and spend my time writing, reading, and painting the old kitchen cupboards. I also organise a new phone number so Jeffrey can't call me.

The cupboards are scuffed, worn, and an ugly shade of green so I sand back the timber and refresh them with the same shade of cream I used for the windowsills. I feel I am getting pro at this reno business, now. I paint the walls of the kitchen a stunning, citrus yellow. The floor is wide plank rimu, and with a thorough mop and scrub, the entire room comes up sparkling.

I am so pleased with it, on Wednesday I call Lori and invite her to a proper, English afternoon tea, just like Mum used to make. I bake fluffy scones, whip some cream, and dole out three different fruit jams into neat little bowls.

Lori turns up on my front lawn after school with her three boys and their dog. I join the boys in a quick, rough and tumble game of tag, then send them off with a basket to look for plums in the orchard.

In the sudden quiet, Lori raises one finely arched eyebrow. "So, sis, what's going on with Linc? He insisted on staying here,

Friday night." She has a wicked tilt to her head and I can't help it, I blush. Then I burst into tears.

Lori rushes over and hugs me. "Nooo, I didn't mean to upset you! So... You like him, but something bad has happened?" She looks at me in confusion, then claps her hand to her mouth. "Oh, lordy, except for the Brad incident, of course. But then, Brad is a complete tosser."

I laugh through my tears. "I'm not upset because of what happened with Brad. It's just that so *much* has happened. I really liked Linc, but I thought he was cheating on his sister, then after the wedding he came and told me he wasn't, and I got together with him. But then Jeffrey rang me and I got scared and I told Linc he had to leave me alone, then Brad asked me out and I couldn't say no, and we all know how badly *that* turned out – and Linc has been so kind, and on the weekend I told Jeffrey to go stuff himself but now I don't know how to make things better with the man I actually really..."

Lori puts her hand up. "Stop! Stop, stop, you left me behind at the bit where you thought Linc was cheating on his sister but he wasn't, then you got together with him. Huh? Run that past me again?"

"I'm sorry. I thought he was cheating on Sue because..."

Lori hoots. "Because he lives with her?" She doubles over, laughing. "Glory, Kate, don't tell too many people that, they'll think you're a few bricks short of a barrow load."

"I think I might be," I grin, and get up to pour the tea. "Let's hope no one but you has noticed."

Lori's expression sobers. "I didn't know Jeffrey had been in contact. Are you OK?"

"Yes." And this time, I mean it. "He wanted money. I told him Mum would turn in her grave if I gave him any, and that I'm changing my number and in future he should contact my lawyer."

Lori's eyes are shining. She claps her hands. "You're a legend, Kate, good on you!"

"But I don't know how to fix things with Linc." I sigh. "Or if I even want to. It all feels like such a mess and I am so, so bad with men. I think I should swear off them forever."

Lori hands me a scone piled high with strawberry jam and way too much cream. "Give yourself time, gorgeous. You've had a hard road to travel in the past few years, you need some time to recover."

"I know." I smile ruefully. "That's why I'm here, living on your farm, in your old house."

"And painting this old kitchen bright yellow!" Lori laughs and hugs me again. "I love that you're here, living near us. And I love that you are looking after this old girl. She's been waiting a long time for someone to care enough to give her a facelift."

I drink my tea, and gaze outside at the weathered old porch, the Waiata gate, and the wet and windblown gardens I have grown to love in all weather. *A facelift*. Hmm, well, there's a bit more work to do yet.

Lori's thoughts are following another path. "You know, Gus says Linc is a really nice bloke but all I see is women throwing themselves at him."

"Yes, women kiss him all the time!" I roll my eyes. Taika runs in, I give him a scone, and he climbs into my lap.

Lori is still musing, "I've always thought, surely that must go to his head? But after seeing Linc in action the other night,

I think I've had your knight in shining armour figured wrong."
I protest, but Lori shakes her head. "No, I'm serious, Kate. He
was so worried about you, he was like a besotted mother hen."

"He made us hot chocolate."

Lori grins. "Correction. He made *you* hot chocolate, and
an extra one for me to be polite!"

Tracing the rim of my teacup with my finger, I say quietly,
"Olive said that Linc loves me. But I didn't believe her at the
time."

Lori's eyebrows go all the way to the roof. "Wow, Kate.
Olive would know. Maybe this is the real thing."

I hug my feelings of hope, sadness, delight and trepidation
to myself, but Lori senses them. She squeezes my hand.
"Darling, give yourself time. If anyone deserves true love and a
happily ever after, it's you. And if Linc is worth it, he'll wait."

"I don't know," I whisper. *He said he would wait, once before,
but I've really hurt him this time.*

Taika has been sitting on my lap all this time, eating, and
kicking his heels on the chair. Nikau and Tommo come tearing
in now for scones and cream, and he loudly declares, "Auntie
Kate is in yuv!"

This goes over Nikau's head, but Tommo considers it for a
moment. "Yuck," he says at last.

"Wiv Yinc!"

"Oh, that's alright then." Tommo nods dismissively, and
Taika jumps down. The boys run off to start a new game,
towing each other up and down the hallway on my best bath
towels.

I gaze at Lori with tears in my eyes and offer her another
cup of tea.

Linc rocks back on his heels to inspect the underside of the landau. He has spent every spare moment in the barn for several weeks now, planing, sanding, oiling, painting and sweating over this old thing until his hands are blistered and his entire body aches. This morning, though, the elegant vehicle looks splendid. Even his mum would be happy with it.

Linc smiles to think of her reaction. She would check the hubs first, in case he'd neglected to grease them. Then she'd trail her fingers over the new, heritage green paintwork and inspect the four iron-shod wheels, trim, straight, and ready for use. He can picture the slow smile and nod of satisfaction she'd offer when she decided it was done right. Yes, she'd be happy. The landau looks perfect.

So, why isn't *he* happy?

Linc rolls his shoulders and straightens up. He doesn't have a matching pair on hand to haul it, like Kate's coachman would. He can't roll it out of a bustling coach house and drive it round to Kate's front door to collect her for a ball, or a country drive – then hold her hand as she steps into the buttoned leather interior. And there, perhaps, is the rub. Is he comparing himself to a fictional coachman from 1790, and coming up short?

Linc gives a sharp bark of a laugh and the fossicking bantam hens scatter from around his feet. "Yes, ladies, run from the madman in your midst." When Dash snorts, too, from her nearby yard, he retorts, "No comment from you, madam, or I'll make you pull this baby all by yourself!" He runs his hands over the landau's fine fretwork for a final check, then steps out into the sunlight, closing the big barn doors behind him.

There are fences to fix, the landscaping team to supervise, and other people's horses to train. Thanks to his weeks-long restoration effort, he is behind in everything else on the farm. And for what? For someone else's idea – someone achingly attractive, who is filling his dreams, plaguing his sleep and distracting his days – but someone, nevertheless, who has made it clear she does not want him close.

Linc frowns and heads for the river terrace. Dick and his crew are scaping new islands into the Reflections pond down there so it will be better for waterbirds. The grey horse is turned out in the Long Paddock nearby, taking a break from training, and he spots Linc. He throws his head up and leads the yearlings in a high-tailed, spirited gallop across the river flats and over the crest towards him. Linc grins, reaching to touch the questing noses and bright eyes of the young horses as they jostle to meet him at the gate.

"It's not dinnertime yet, boys, go back and eat more grass."

It is a typical, early autumn day, with sunlight chasing fitful showers followed by leaf-skittering wind. Linc lifts his face to the sun in time to see Olive's car come over the brow of Sundial Hill. She has driven across country from her little house in Lori's olive grove. Her car lurches across the rough grass, her huskies streaming out ahead of her, running with wild exuberance, their tails joyous flags against the sky.

This revving, bumping, barking cacophony rounds the Sundial lawn, pours down the hill and arrives messily in front of Linc. As the dogs fan out around him to explore, Olive winds down her window.

"I've been thinking about you," she calls.

"Darling, I thought you'd never ask."

"Not like that, you naughty man," Olive laughs. "I mean, about you and Kate."

"There *is* no me and Kate."

"Lori came over last night. She said Kate's ex contacted her, a few weeks ago. Kate told him to get lost, but it really shook her up."

Linc stares. *That's why she looked so scared*. He bites his lip. *And that's why she ran*. For the first time, it occurs to him that Kate's rejection might have nothing to do with him or their awkward lovemaking. He runs his hand over his jaw, and frowns.

Stupid. I've been stupid, thinking this was about me. His recent heartbreak and jealousy now seem shallow and petty. Yes, she has hurt him, but he's never been hurt in the ways Kate has.

"You need to give her time, Linc." Olive is watching him. "Remember your horses? You step back and let them come in, in their own time."

For a fleeting moment, Linc looks lost. "It's been weeks. What if she doesn't come in?"

Olive forces a smile. "I can't help you there, Lincoln darling, but I have hope for you. You'll work it out. As your mother always said, you can't be that pretty for nothing!" She tips her chin in farewell, and whistles for her dogs. "Come on you lot, we're going home."

With a jolt and a scrape, Olive drives forward over the edge of the yew walk. She pirouettes her little car on the immaculate gravel, bumps back over the side and roars off up the hill. Her dogs circle Linc, sniffing, then give tongue and hurtle up the slope after their mistress.

The grey horse had been standing off while the dogs were nearby. Now, he comes up to the gate and nudges Linc.

"I know. I was dumb, young fella. I thought it was all about me." *But it's not. So, maybe she'll forgive me and let me kiss her again. In about fifty years' time, when I've found a way to talk to her that won't scare her off.* Linc scratches the grey around the ears. "By then I'll be ninety-three and frail, and unable to make the most of it. And you'll be long gone. Them's the breaks, boy." Linc tugs at the knotted silver forelock, then strides off to find Dick and his digger.

After watching the digger for half an hour or so, Linc realises he doesn't have to go in person to invite Kate to see the landau. He could write an invitation to her. Perhaps that would accommodate both Olive's advice to give her space, and his own desperate desire to see her.

Chapter 17

I am deeply absorbed in oiling the Waiata gate when I hear a familiar cacophony coming up the driveway. I turn with a smile on my lips in the clouded afternoon light, to see Olive and the huskies sweep into view, three besotted, yelling boys pedalling behind.

I haven't been to the café for a few weeks now, as I felt I needed some time to myself. This has translated into frenzied bouts of writing, and sanding, oiling and painting any timber surfaces in sight. The homestead is now looking spick and span, and the last thing to finish is the gate.

Olive is grinning from ear to ear as she approaches, urging her dogs to greater speed. "Hellooo, Kate!" she yodels, as she hurtles by. "Lovely to see you!"

"Hello!" I wave, and watch her disappear, and in a moment the boys are upon me. I snatch up my pot of oil as they crash in a collective tangle at the base of the Waiata gate, spinning wheels and handlebars everywhere.

"Hi auntie Kate!" they chorus, climbing out miraculously intact. "Hayyo!"

"Hello, darlings."

"Why is you fixing da gate?" Taika wants to know.

"Because it is old and needs looking after."

"Dad is old, so we need to look after him," Tommo says. The twins agree. I laugh and assure them their father is not particularly old, although it's still a nice idea to look after him. *Because blimey, if Gus is old, how ancient does that make me?*

I ignore the old palpitations of anxiety welling up and fix myself firmly in the moment. Here are the twins standing before me, fidgeting, their big, bright eyes looking into my face. And here is Tommo, the sensible elder brother, trying to shepherd them back onto their bicycles.

There is a brief flurry as they disentangle all the wheels and pedals, and locate Taika's exploded helmet. As Taika clips the scuffed top and bottom layers back together and wedges it askew on his head, Tommo fishes an envelope from his pocket.

"I nearly forgot, auntie Kate. This is from Linc."

"Yinc sended you a yuv yetter," nods Taika, grinning.

"No," Tommo turns on him with scorn. "It's not a love letter. It's an invitation. That's what Linc said."

"Dere's no yuv in it," Nikau agrees, mournfully.

More's the pity. But I take the letter and thank them, and the boys hurtle off, bickering and yelling, in hectic pursuit of the dogs.

I sit down by the Waiata gate with my heart in my mouth. What does Linc have to say to me?

Linc's envelope contains a single sheet of paper and a scatter of dried rose petals. In a light scrawl, Linc has written, 'Kate, I hope you are well. Please come to Summer H. tomorrow afternoon at two. I have something to show you.' It is signed with an unintelligible flourish, beneath which is written, 'The grey horse says hello.'

That horse. He really needs a name. Oh, and that man. I lean my head against the gate with a sigh. I will forever be a slave to him. Because, though I've made a fool of myself time after time around him, and hurt and confused him inexcusably, Linc has invited me to his house, and I will go. How can I refuse? I will go, in a flutter of hope and infatuation, if only to bask in his chocolate gaze again.

It is one in the afternoon and Linc is pacing the front verandah. Sue is nearby, photographing raindrops beading on the leaves of the rose bushes.

She looks up from her work, strands of hair plastered across her face. "Go away Linc, you're distracting me. Haven't you got horses to train or something?"

"Done already. I'll get the grey out again later."

"Well, go and play with your cars, you're in the way here." She pauses. "What are you doing, anyway? You look like you're waiting for someone."

"Kate is coming at two to see the landau."

Sue sits up. "Ooh, how nice!"

Linc gives her a look, and Sue grins. "I mean that in the nicest possible way. This time though, you have to introduce me properly."

Linc is about to reply when there is the crunch of tyres on gravel and a silver hatchback appears. He groans. "What is *she* doing here?"

Sue looks up from her camera. "Who?"

"Mira!"

"I asked her advice on some packaging designs." Sue sees Linc's expression. "Oh, hell. Sorry. I'll try to keep her out of the way, alright?"

Linc grunts. "I'll be in the shed." He strides away towards the big car garage, taking the side verandah so Mira can't catch a glimpse of him.

Sue sighs. She puts her camera away and musters a cheery smile. "Mira, great timing, I was just about to put the kettle on!"

I knock on the leadlight front door of the villa, and Mira opens it. Her smile freezes. "Hi, Kate. What are you doing here?"

My heart gives a lurch and I gape at her. Has Mira moved up out of the 'friend' zone while I've been painting my house? I'm not surprised at her, but I am disappointed Linc is not languishing after me. The irony of that, when it was me who dumped him, leads me to stifle a laugh.

I bite back my fledgling bitterness and proceed with a casualness I do not feel. "Hello, Mira. Um, Linc invited me here to look at something."

Mira raises an interrogative brow and I realise how that sounds. "Oh. I mean, it might have something to do with horses. Probably." I am digging myself a metaphorical hole here, with no rescue horse in sight.

Linc appears abruptly round the side of the villa, rubbing at his hands with a cloth. He stops short at the sight of Mira and I, standing together on the verandah. "Kate." He smiles. "You're early."

Save me. "If you're busy, I can just…"

"No, please, follow me." Linc jams the greasy cloth in his pocket and walks off. Mira looks like she might come too, but Sue calls her from somewhere in the villa and she disappears inside.

I follow. I drink in the sight of Linc's lean, muscled frame as I trail behind him. He leads me past the horse yards, where we give Dash a quick pat, then over to the biggest of the outbuildings behind the villa. He swings open big double doors with a groan of ancient hinges, and I follow him inside. The huge barn is cool and draughty, with a cavernous, gabled ceiling. Chinks of light show between rough-sawn timber planks.

I am entranced by the massive roof beams inside, the dancing light, and the golden stacks of hay. It occurs to me that if I had found this place as a child, I'd never have left. I'd have climbed into that hay with a book and a blanket and stayed forever, breathing in the grassy scent, reading, and dreaming of horses.

Then, I realise why Linc has brought me here. "Ohhh..."

Linc is watching me with his chocolate eyes. "I thought it might help with your book."

"Oh, yes, and it's beautiful!" I run my fingers along the shining carriage with its ornate little step, brass lanterns and gently curved shafts. I can imagine my splendidly-dressed Hattie being handed into this vehicle by her coachman. Who is, of course, Linc. Just a little older, and much, much more accessible. "Linc, it is lovely! Where did you find it?"

Linc shrugs. "It was here when my grandfather took over the farm. My mother restored it thirty years ago, and it's been sitting around since then. When you asked about harness driving a few weeks ago, it occurred to me I should tidy it up."

"Well, you've done an amazing job." The finely-sprung vehicle is gleaming, from its hubcaps to its two brass lanterns, to the fine timber scrollwork around the elevated driver's seat. I feel alive, alight at the possibilities, my story humming to life in my head.

Linc steps close, running his hands, too, along the paintwork. "This is a landau," he says, his voice husky. "It can be used as an enclosed carriage, or run with the top down. It is usually pulled by two horses, so in your Lady Hatwick's day I reckon the wealthy families with multiple horses would own them. Your average Joe would run a gig or a dray."

I look into his face. He is very close. *Does he want to touch me? Please, please, I want him to touch me.* I cram Hattie's wanton thoughts to the back of my mind. "Um. Two horses?"

"A pair of horses, harnessed abreast, with reins running back here to the driver," he indicates with his hands. "To pull well together, the horses need a similar length of stride, so they'll usually be matched in height and build. In the case of your rich lady, they'd be matched in colour and markings, too."

"Could you drive it?"

Linc meets my gaze. "Yes. Dash is ready, but the grey will be a few months yet."

I smile to think that the landau might one day be used again. I circle it, and marvel. The sight and smell of Linc this close is intoxicating. I want to drag this clever, gorgeous man inside the buttoned leather interior and shower sweet, passionate kisses on him. But it is too late for that. Mira answered the door to his house today, so he is definitely not here to kiss me.

I admire the landau, and Linc watches me, and we circle each other politely in the still, warm air of the barn. It is not until we are leaving that I realise he has remembered my heroine's name. Is it possible he has restored the landau for me?

The thought makes me breathless. *Could he be thinking of you, Katie, like you are thinking of him?*

I shush my mother's voice and follow Linc out of the barn into the blustery wind. We cross the yard and mount the rear steps of the villa. There is a large utilities room, where he offers me soap and a towel to wash up. Our fingers meet over the laundry tub and I feel the quick, familiar burn when we touch.

"Sorry." I snatch my hand away.

Linc clears his throat. "I'll take you to see Sue, if you don't mind. She wanted to say hi."

Feeling a tremor of anxiety, I nod, and we walk together along a corridor as wide as my dining room. There are paintings on the papered walls, and one of them stops me in my tracks. "Blimey, don't tell me she paints, too?"

Linc pauses midstride. "Who?"

"Your sister." I am stricken. "She must be the ultimate Renaissance woman."

He glances over and flashes a grin. "No. My mother did that, about a year before she died. She wanted to paint me working one of her colts. She bred warmblood mares with our stationbred stallion and got some very good performance horses on the ground." He says something about Dash being the last filly his mother bred, but I am transfixed by the painting and barely hear.

"It's an excellent likeness." Gazing at the canvas, I can see just how well Linc's mother understood him. She has captured his light stance in the yard, his calm, laser focus on the horse, his strong hands riding gently on the rope. Her intuition, perception, and love for her son radiates from every brushstroke.

My heart aches for his loss, and for mine. Neither of us has parents left living, and I have an even greater hole looming before me, for I have lost Linc.

As though she reads my mind, Mira breezes back into view. She takes Linc's arm and smiles at him. "There you are! Sue says coffee is ready in the Blue Room." As an afterthought, Mira's gaze flicks to me. "Sue wants to show you her orchids, Kate. She says some of them came from the Waiata garden." She looks into Linc's eyes. "Isn't that right, Lincoln?"

Linc is looking daggers about something, but I have no time to wonder what. I am struck by instant panic at the thought of having to share coffee and smalltalk with Sue, Linc and Mira. Together. In a Blue Room, of all places.

"I think–" I stammer, "I think I have to go." I glance at Linc and say, again, "I'm sorry." And I am. About everything. Especially about not kissing him today on those buttoned leather seats.

Linc slips his arm from Mira's and follows me to the door. "Kate, I..."

"Linc, the landau is lovely, I'm so glad I saw it. It will help me with my story." I keep my head down so he can't see my tears. I want to smile at him brightly, dazzle him, whisk him away from Mira and kiss him until he forgets her – until he thinks he could love me again. Even just a little bit.

Linc, I love you. I love the landau, the horses, your mother's painting, your sister's attention to detail, that burbling old ute of yours and, well, pretty much everything about you.

But I cannot speak without crying, so I slide into Lori's car and wave a cheery goodbye that I do not feel. As I enter the tree-lined drive, I check the rearview mirror. Linc is no longer at the door. I am that easily forgotten.

Linc stares after the car, struck by overwhelming frustration. He rounds on Mira. "You have to stop doing that, Mira, you know I like Kate!"

Mira's eyes grow big. "Linc, baby, I don't know what you're talking about."

"I am not your Linc baby!" Linc growls. He leaps down the stairs, hurdles the decorative garden gate and sprints round the villa to the yards. Dash jerks up her head, her ears pricked, and whickers a welcome as he throws open the gate.

"Come on, girl, let's go." Linc crosses the yard in two strides and vaults onto the mare's back. He grasps a fistful of mane and touches his heels to her sides. Bareback and bridleless, Dash responds instantly to his touch. She leaps forward, kicking out gravel as she rounds the gatepost, and they gallop out across the big paddock towards the highway.

Dash's head stretches into the wind and her russet tail flows behind her as she speeds for the road. Linc catches glimpses of Kate's car moving between the trees parallel to him, winding down the long, villa drive and pulling up at the intersection to the main road. He sets Dash at the boundary fence and she clears it easily, then he asks for a tight left turn. She gallops the short distance, Linc leans back and she comes to a sliding, cowboy-style halt in front of Kate's car.

Linc sees Kate's stunned expression as Dash and he arrive suddenly in view. There is a slight frown at her brow and he feels desperation, impending failure, a tiny spark of hope. He touches his right heel to Dash's side and sidles her to Kate's open window.

"Kate." He leans down to look at her. Oh, those beautiful green eyes. *Has she been crying?* "Kate, I need to tell you. I know what this looks like, but... Mira is here to see Sue, not me. I didn't even know she was coming."

Kate looks shocked, and her eyes fill with tears. *Yes, she is definitely crying.* He wants to wrap his arms around her and love her, but there is a horse, a car door and a million miles between them. He must not push her, he knows. Olive was right.

He rustles up a smile. "Sweet as. Well, I... just wanted you to know." Kate still doesn't say anything, so he swings Dash about and lopes her home, the mare's hooves crunching a four-beat rhythm on the gravel drive, solemn enough to match his heart.

When he looks back over his shoulder, Kate is still sitting in her car, staring ahead. Slowly, very slowly, she eases forward onto the highway and turns left towards Waiata.

Chapter 18

I arrive home filled with restlessness, confusion, and an unaccountable sense of failure. There is a final post on the Waiata gate which needs oiling, so I finish this before darkness falls. I take a long, hot shower to wash off the sawdust, oil, and my bizarre sense of ennui, then stand nonplussed in my pyjamas in the hall. My evening stretches before me with depressive solemnity. I grab a tub of chocolate icecream, wrap myself in a blanket, and watch three rom coms in a row before falling asleep on the couch.

The phone rings and I leap awake at some ungodly hour, well before dawn. My head is filled with dreams of Dash galloping, and Linc's quizzical smile, and it takes me a moment to get my bearings. "Hello?"

My lawyer's voice is breathless. "Kate, have you seen the news from London? There's been an accident. I'm so sorry for your loss. But Jeffrey put his assets in your name for tax purposes, so you're about to become a very rich woman."

"Huh?" I struggle up, dragging the blanket with me, and pad through the connecting doors to my laptop in the next room. I open a search browser, type in Jeffrey's full name, and am bombarded with page after page of sensational headlines and images of a fiery car crash.

"A car crash?" My heart is pounding and my throat is dry. This all seems so ridiculous. Impossible.

"My contacts have confirmed he was in the car, and that the body at the morgue is Jeffrey. He was driving inebriated, too fast, and failed to make a corner. You will inherit everything he owned, Kate. Jeffrey's business assets have been frozen, but he has a luxury property in London and a villa in France, both listed in your name. His family may make a fuss, but you are his wife and he never recognised the separation so your claim is good." I can hear Amber smiling over the phone. "I'll get onto the necessary paperwork and be in touch soon."

"Oh. Thankyou." Amber closes the call, and in the sudden silence I stare blankly at my computer screen. Odd, fragmented thoughts whirl through my mind. *If I have enough money, perhaps I can help Lori's family and Gus won't have to work so hard. I could set up a trust and rescue horses. Or dogs, because Mum loved dogs. Perhaps I could buy this homestead.* Then it hits me. *I am a widow.*

I am still sitting, stunned, at 4am. I can't believe it. I have had the strangest day and it is not over yet. I read the Times obituary again and again, the solemn words describing the sudden death of the Earl's youngest son, along with a bare, impersonal description of the Honorable Jeffrey's numerous professional achievements and awards.

My mind inserts a subtext for each date – that's the night he hit me because I wouldn't get into the car with him drunk; that's the awards evening when he went home with Lady Petra instead of me, and didn't turn up again for three days; that's the career move that took us to Australia and which he found so stressful that he hit the bottle, and me, every night for two years. I can count Jeffrey's professional career in the scars on my body and the broken edges of my heart. I can trace his life in the lake of pain he left me.

And now he's gone.

I didn't realise until I read his obituary how sure I've been that one day he will come back. How frightened I've been, beneath my veneer of a new start, that he might destroy everything I've built. Tear down my healing. Shatter my peace.

Taunt me about my mother's death, how I'm all alone now and I need him.

It isn't until I discover Jeffrey is dead that I discover this tension nestled in my soul. Is this why I've been so up and down, light and shade, carrying a 'shadow', as Lori called it? Is this why I've been clinging to Linc, a man I met just a few months ago, like a woman drowning?

I cannot possibly know. Discovering Jeffrey is gone forever has rocked me. I feel all the hurt, pain, anger, betrayal and hatred come flooding back.

I am in no fit state in the morning to go to the bookshop with Olive when she drives up and toots her horn. I stay beneath the covers in Bluebell, and she eventually goes away. I stay there all day, cocooned with my strange, twisted grief.

Hunger and thirst drive me out at sunset.

The sky is clear and the setting sun casts a pink and orange shawl over the horizon, but I cannot feel her comfort. I sit, feeling frozen and disjointed, nursing a glass of water and a leftover slice of lasagna. There is no microwave in the homestead and I can't face cooking so I eat it cold, watching the dusk gather in deepening folds about the garden. I am plagued by memories. I wish there was someone to call but I have no friends left from my life with Jeffrey, my mum is gone, and Lori never actually met him.

What did it matter anyway? What did any of it matter, it was all so warped and abusive. There'd been no hope for our marriage, no hope for him, and now no hope for me because I am still broken. I had hoped I was healing but I see that these feelings have come back so strong today, so awesome in their twisted power, I am terrified the last few years were all for nothing.

I leave my plate outside on the wrought iron bench, patter barefoot down the hall and slide back into Bluebell's bed. I feel better in the dark, with the covers over me.

Olive brings reinforcements the next morning. I hear Lori's voice calling me, and they both skirt the perimeter of my house, tripping over garden edging, knocking on windows until they locate me in the Bluebell room.

Lori peers in through the glass, the morning light creating a bright halo about her head. "Kate, what's the matter? Are you alright?"

I wave one hand from beneath my quilt, but I don't come out. "I'm alive. Just go away." I don't want her to see my puffy eyes and my stupid tears over my bastard of an ex. *What is wrong with me?*

Lori sounds concerned. "What's going on, Kate? Please tell me."

I know my sister, she is so determined she might stay there all day, so I mutter just loud enough for her to hear, "Jeffrey is dead."

"Oh, lordy."

Yes. Now please leave me to my warm cocoon here, I can't talk to you today.

My plea is silent but heartfelt, and they do, but in the evening I find a pot of warm chicken soup has been left on my kitchen bench. I cry more tears, this time of appreciation, eat some soup and go to sleep in Sunflower. Maybe things are looking up. Or maybe I just can't face sleeping in those sodden sheets in Bluebell anymore.

The next day, Linc arrives. He sits in the back porch and hums a melodic, wordless song to Dash while I lie still, listening to him, and the morning sun dances leaf shadows across my ceiling. I can hear Dash tearing up mouthfuls of the long grass behind my house. I find the gentle sounds of her eating, her occasional soft snort and the swish of her tail oddly comforting.

I think of the last time I saw her. Of her beautiful, sliding stop in front of my car, the desperation in Linc's eyes, and my strange, silent, frozen heart.

After what feels like an hour or more, I creep out and open the back door. I know I still look like death, but somehow right now I don't care.

Linc and I look at each other for a long moment. At last, he says, "Lori sent me. Are you OK?"

"I don't know."

"Do you need anything? Anyone?"

"I don't know," I whisper. "Maybe my mum?"

Linc flashes a brief grin. "Not sure I can help you there." He pats the firewood beside him, and I slide down to sit on the woodpile.

"I think maybe it's time I grew up anyway," I say, sadly. He is so close I can feel his body heat, but we do not touch.

"Oh, I don't know, Kate. I think growing up is overrated. I try to do it as little as possible."

As always, I find it impossible to stay down in Linc's company. He exudes calm and warmth, his irrepressible humour bubbling just under the surface. Just sitting beside him today is enough to lift my mood.

Linc stretches out his legs, leans back against the weatherboards and tips his hat over his eyes. I watch Dash eating my grass, the fantails flitting above the lawn, the slow burn of the sun as the shadows shorten and the world marches on towards lunchtime.

I've been here before. Somehow, Linc has become the one I lean on. And I've done an unusual lot of it lately, even for me.

Eventually I tell him, "Jeffrey died."

"I heard."

"I don't know why I'm sad about it. He was a total and utter bastard."

Linc is grim. "My dad and I couldn't be in the same room without arguing. But I was still upset when he died."

"Were you?" I look at him. He meets my gaze with a crooked grin, and he looks resigned rather than sad. I think about that for a while, and feel a weight begin to lift. "You know, Linc, that actually makes me feel better. Where have you been all my life?"

Linc leans over. He tilts my chin to meet his. He traces two fingers down the side of my face to my lips, long and slow. His touch is full of healing, lightning and promise, all in one, and I am left breathless.

"Right here," he says. "Waiting for you."

Chapter 19

I stare at him. Linc's fingertips linger on my mouth for a moment, then he gives a lopsided smile and turns away to watch Dash.

I am frozen with doubt and grief, but I feel Linc's words go in deep and settle. They rest there like a warm talisman against the anxiety and sadness that is eating me. Linc watches his horse, and breathes beside me, and I watch the horse too, in my frozen daydream. I feel my heartbeat slowing, quieting, easing into synch with that little talisman.

After a time, Linc gets up, kisses the top of my head in silent farewell, and leads Dash away through the Waiata gate. He will ride home, feed his animals, perhaps spend some time training the grey. I sit a few moments more on the woodpile, thinking of the talisman inside me.

Right here. Waiting for you.

There is a quiet strength and a quiet trust, a million years and a lifetime of love in those words. I wonder if I dare hope it could all be for me.

I think about the space between us. I realise I am now more afraid of that than I am of Jeffrey. I don't want it between us anymore. *Jeffrey is dead, Katie. Linc is real. He is safe and kind, and he loves you.* I run my fingers over my scars and feel a cold, hard carapace settle around the memories of Jeffrey. There is that scar on my shoulder, the small one behind my ear, the defensive cut on the inside of my right arm.

Jeffrey is dead. Jeffrey the bastard. Jeffrey the gone. My relief is palpable, my thoughts unprintable.

I realise that I have it all right and all wrong at the same time. I need Linc *now*, not tomorrow, next week, or next year. I know he is being patient and kind, but I am suddenly, hopelessly overwhelmed by the feeling that I need him. Now. Forever.

I leap up from the woodpile, trip over the back step and scramble through the Waiata gate. "Linc!" I scream, and there is hope and fear and desperation in my voice. It is reflected in his expression as he reins Dash around.

"I'm sorry, Linc, I should never have let you go. Not now. Not ever." I am running down the driveway towards him, and he is looking at me quizzically. Even Dash has a bemused look in her eyes. "Linc, please! I want you. Jeffrey is gone and I've had it all wrong, grieving like that when we could be so much more..."

I've reached them now. Linc swings off his horse and catches me in his arms. "Bloody hell, Kate," he says hoarsely, "I was afraid you'd never work it out."

I pause. He is holding me tight. Are there tears in his eyes? "I'm sorry, I have been so slow. When I think of how you came to my door weeks ago and said you liked me, but then Jeffrey called and I..."

He puts his fingers to my lips. "Stop apologising."

"But I should have trusted you and explained, instead I..."

"Kate. Please."

"Then the other day you and Dash... uh, OK." I stop gabbling, and just gaze at him.

"I'm sorry too, my love," Linc says softly. "I didn't try hard enough to find out what went wrong with us."

I am still gazing. *My love.* He studies my face for a long moment. Perhaps he is as transfixed as I am. Then I blink. Being impulsive and chasing him down the driveway is all very well, but I realise I haven't showered in days and I must look a mess.

Self-consciously, I step back, brush down my dress and try to tidy my hair.

He flashes a grin. "How about I take Dash home and come back in an hour? We can make dinner together."

"Oh, yes. Yes!" But I don't have dinner in mind. I am calculating how long it will take me to change the sheets in Sunflower, find my best lingerie, and wrangle my hair into something more civilised than a bird's nest. And somewhere deep in the back of my mind, I am crafting a white-hot sex scene between Hattie and her coachman, and a secret inheritance for her so she can leave her husband, live independently in a large, country estate and have her handsome coachman on tap.

When Linc kicks his boots off in the porch that afternoon and opens the back door, I meet him dressed only in panties and get him up against the wall before he's even had a chance to say hello.

I crush Linc's lips against mine and slide my hand inside his jeans. I feel his whole body harden up and wrap around me. He lifts me to eye level and says, through my breathless, nipping kisses, "Hi, Kate, have I missed something?"

"Not really, but I've missed you. Bedroom. Now." I want to start again where we left off, weeks ago.

"You sure?"

"Yes, yes, and yes. Definitely."

"Sweet," Linc grins. He kicks the door shut with his foot, and sweeps me down the hall and into Sunflower.

"I want you," I whisper. I drag his tee up over his head, undo his jeans, trail my fingers over his flexing muscles as he kicks off his clothes and is naked at last. I feel his breath, his body against mine, taste his mouth and the salt on his skin. I know he wants me, and the joy and desire inside me is so fierce it hurts.

I guide his hands upwards and gasp as he traces the curve of my breast, my swollen nipples, my throat, tangles his fingers in my mouth and in my hair. His body is hard against mine, his jawline rough and bristled, his teeth gentle but urgent as they nip my skin.

I move my thigh between his, rubbing, inviting, feeling him harden and swell. He breathes faster as I press against him. I can feel his edges and mine dissolving as we move together. He is still bare, throbbing against my thigh, so he rummages now in his jeans pocket, rolls on a condom and we share a smile. I hold his gaze and wet my lips with my tongue. He moans softly and cups my breasts with his palms, rubs his thumb over my nipples, teases me with his tongue, licks and tantalises me until I am breathless with heat and need.

I slide my fingers down, push him onto the bed, part my legs and slip astride his thighs. My breasts feel pendulous, my skin radiant, my body slick with wanting. He looks at me with eyes of darkness, his voice thick with desire as he groans, "Oh,

Kate." He rests his warm hands on my hips, pulsing muscle between us.

I move slowly, teasingly, against him. He pulls me down so my breasts brush his chest, and lightly kisses the scar on my shoulder, but I have no hesitation this time. My hands are at his back, my mouth is lost against his. Linc and I move together, skin against skin, flame meeting fire, both of us wet and writhing. We ride a passionate wave, his lust receptive to mine, his overwhelming desire to pleasure me. He rubs against me, his fingers tease and command me, he brings me, gasping, to that place I want to share with him.

After, still trembling, I tumble over and bring him round with me. His shoulders are silhouetted against the ceiling now, his eyes on mine as he gently, hesitantly, eases inside me. He is being careful, I love him for it but I want more. I make a small sound of pleasure and wrap my legs about him, driving him deeper. Linc begins cautiously to move, but as I gasp and clench him harder he thrusts more urgently. My body arches to meet his, both of us slick and pumping, our blood hot and pulsing. We become one, lost inside each other, and cry out as we climax together.

We roll, spent and satisfied, across the bed. He has one hand beneath me, my legs are entwined with his. Our heated breathing slows. I lift my face to his and he smiles, slow and warm, his teeth flashing white in the darkness.

"Thankyou," he says, "I didn't imagine this today." I bury my face in his chest, and he wraps me in his embrace. "Was it research for your book?" There is laughter behind the words and I know Linc is keeping the mood light, skating around the big questions. There will be time enough for them.

"Absolutely," I grin. "But you know, they might do it differently in the 1800's."

"More practice is needed, then?"

"Definitely." I snuggle into him.

"Anytime, Kate. Although maybe give me a minute..." I laugh at his rueful expression and we cuddle, drawing up the sheets.

After a moment, I think of something. "Linc?"

"Mm."

"You could call your grey horse Waiata."

"It's a good name."

I listen to Linc's breathing slow and deepen, and feel the old homestead wrap her silence gently, approvingly about us. I feel safe here, warm and healed. I love this place and this man.

Later, I get up and write a final scene of slow, gentle lovemaking. This is a wrap-up scene where Hattie and her man bring their lives and love together so Hattie can go on and forge a new path with him, as only this tempestuous, voluptuous, mightily determined woman can.

"What are you doing?" Linc's voice is sleepy.

"Lady Hatwick's coachman is showing her how much he loves her."

"I think you need applied research for that one. Come back to bed, beautiful."

I think about that for precisely point three milliseconds. "OK." I slap my laptop shut. I stand up and let my robe slide to the floor. The smooth silk slips down over my breast and thigh and I feel my nipples swell erect, my belly flutter hotly in the cool night air.

Linc is stretched across my sheets, moonlight dappled over his muscled flanks, his dark eyes hungry. I slide into bed alongside him and he meets me at my mouth and groin, tangling one leg strongly about me, his hand over my buttocks drawing me close.

I lose myself in his touch.

The following Monday, I am back at Olive's coffee machine. The chrome still sparkles, the milk still froths and the scent of roasted beans is the same, but everything else is different. I am walking on a cloud, and humming, and Olive is looking at me meditatively.

"You are very happy today, Kate."

"Yes." I hand Daisy's mochaccino with extra sugar through the serving window, and scoop her ginger kitten from halfway up the net curtains. "Oops, Daisy. Here, take your runaway with you." I return the wayward feline, and Daisy potters off down the wind-skittered street.

"I'm pleased you're feeling better."

"Yes." I smile as I wipe down the coffee bench and count off the seconds in my head, because I know Olive is itching to ask and she won't be able to...

"Did Linc manage to drop by and see you?"

Five, I think to myself. *Does everyone know everything in this town?*

"Yes," says Linc, appearing at the coffee window. He looks fresh and warm and as energetic as I feel, and I want to climb over the counter and kiss him.

My smile widens. I tuck away a stray lock of hair and say, "Coffee?"

"In a minute." Linc leans over the servery bench, lifts me as though I am a featherweight and kisses me. My feet are off the ground, my belly is pressed against the sill, but his hands feel strong and safe. He tastes divine and I lean in, giving a low, guttural sound of pleasure as he deepens the kiss.

My edges dissolve, nothing else exists...

"Oh, my," says Olive.

"Oooh," squeals Billie, from across the courtyard. "Can I come and work for you, Olive? I'm in the wrong business, no one kisses *me* like that."

Linc puts me down and grins. "Hello, beautiful."

"Hi." I am breathless. I can still feel his hands on me, his mouth on mine, and I flush to think that half the town may have seen us. I straighten my dress just as the bell on the front door jangles and a double whirlwind enters the shop.

"Hayyo, auntie Kate, we seed you kissing Yinc!"

"Yay, Yinc yuvs you!"

"Yuck," says Tommo, strolling in after the twins.

I turn to meet Lori's eyes, which are shining with happy tears, and catch Taika with one hand before he can eat the sugar. With the other, I reach blindly for Linc. He wraps his warm fingers around mine and presses my hand to his heart.

Linc, my love, hold me. Forever will not be too long.

Author's Note

This story was written for mature readers. It pays homage to my love of horses, old homesteads, bands and Happily Ever Afters! My characters are condensed from my years living in small towns, playing in bands, caring for animals, towing small children about, losing my purpose and finding it again – all the messy, marvellous mayhem of life!

References to abuse are provided in the context of Kate's healing journey to hope, trust and love. Coffee-related terms are from Down Under – a long black, Linc's favourite, is an Americano made extra strong by adding less water. It is the only coffee my husband drinks, a habit forged while working on submarines. Because Aotearoa New Zealand is a bilingual country with a rich Māori heritage, I have also included some commonly used words from Te Reo Māori.

Ab.

Acknowledgements

This book would not be possible without the trailblazing efforts of my talented friends in Romance Writers New Zealand. Also the support of my husband, who has learned to roll over and snooze in sympathy when I'm up writing feverishly at 3AM. My story has benefitted immeasurably from the critical eye of my talented sister Megan, and test reading by Helen and Jack. Thankyou, as always.

Linc's horsemanship and Olive's huskies come from the adventures of my remarkable friend Glenys who, along with my lovely friends Clara and Lorene, have transformed my understanding of horse behaviour and training. Lori's busy little boys sprang naturally from the chaos our four children brought to our home over the years. Yes, boys, I left out that story about you setting fire to the woodpile. And no, I don't promise to leave it out of future books.

Lastly, thankyou to my readers. There is a new Abigail Bay book hot on the heels of this one, so I'll see you again soon!

About the Author

Abigail Bay writes about people, animals, and the gorgeous, messy mayhem of life and love. She has also written scientific papers, short stories and songs. Abbie lives with her family in a bushclad valley in Aotearoa New Zealand.

Read more at https://www.abigailbay.com.